CROWNED: AN ORDINARY GIRL

CROWNED: AN ORDINARY GIRL

BY

NATASHA OAKLEY

MILLS & BOON®

First published in Great Britain 2006
Large Print edition 2007
Harlequin Mills & Boon Limited,
Eton House, 18-24 Paradise Road,
Richmond, Surrey TW9 1SR

© Natasha Oakley 2006

ISBN-13: 978 0 263 19462 3

Set in Times Roman 16½ on 19 pt.
16-0607-51248

Printed and bound in Great Britain
by Antony Rowe Ltd, Chippenham, Wiltshire

CHAPTER ONE

'YOU'RE reading Chekhov. Have you read any Tolstoy?'

Dr Marianne Chambers hesitated midway through the second paragraph of the paper she was proofreading. A small frown pulled at the centre of her forehead as she recognised the uncanny echo of a long-ago conversation.

It had to be impossible. Why would *he* be at the Cowper Hotel during an academic conference? She was being completely ridiculous.

But…

The memory of that sunny afternoon tugged at her and her frown deepened. It was the same upper-class English accent, with the same hint of something indefinably 'foreign' about it.

And *exactly* the same words.

Marianne remembered them verbatim. In fact, she remembered every single blasted thing Seb

Rodier had ever said to her—from the first moment he'd seen her reading Chekhov on the steps of Amiens Cathedral.

A shadow fell across her page and the voice behind her continued. 'Or Thomas Hardy? Now, he can be really depressing, but if you like that kind of thing…'

Dear God, no.

Marianne's head whipped round to look directly up into a calmly smiling face. Older, more determined maybe, but still the face of the man who'd completely derailed her life.

Back then he'd worn old jeans and a comfortable T-shirt, seemingly an exchange student like herself. Now he stood there in a designer suit and smelt of seriously old money.

There was no surprise in that. She must have seen several hundred newspaper photographs of Prince Sebastian II over the years, but not one of them had prepared her for the overwhelming sense of…*yearning* she felt as she met his dark eyes.

'Hello, Marianne,' he said softly.

Seb!

His name imploded in her head, while every

single moment she'd spent with him all those summers before came whizzing back into high-definition clarity.

Every dream.

Every heartbreak.

In the space of a millisecond she felt as though she'd been sucked back in time. Just eighteen years old. A long way from home and living with a family she barely knew. She'd been so scared, so very scared. Waiting for him. Hoping for a telephone call…

Anything.

Wanting to understand what was happening. Wanting him. Desperately wanting *him*.

She'd wondered how this moment might feel. Not that she'd ever anticipated she'd find out. He'd left…and their paths had never crossed again.

And why would they? Lowly paid academics didn't often run into members of the aristocracy, let alone an honest-to-goodness blue blooded royal.

'Seb?' It was difficult to force the words past the blockage in her throat. 'Sh-should I call you that? Or is it Your Highness? Or…Your Royal

Highness? I don't know what I—' Marianne reached up a hand to brush at the sharp pain stabbing in her forehead.

He moved closer and spoke quietly. 'Your Serene Highness, but Seb will do. It's good to see you. How have you been?'

Somewhere in the background Marianne could hear the sound of laughter and the clink of tea-spoons on china. Incongruous sounds of normality as everything around her started to spin.

'Fine. I've been fine,' she lied. 'And you?'

'Fine.' Seb moved round to stand in front of her. 'It's been a very long time.'

'Yes.'

He paused, his brown eyes seeming to melt her body from the toes up. 'You look amazing. Really amazing.'

'Th-thank you. So do you.' *Damn!* 'I mean…you look…' She trailed off, uncertain of anything—except that she really couldn't do this. Whatever *this* was.

'May I sit beside you?'

No!

What was he *doing*? They weren't merely friends who'd happened to bump into each other.

Far from it. She might not have much experience of meeting 'old' lovers, but surely you didn't sit there making conversation as though you didn't know exactly what the other looked like naked?

Marianne shuffled the typed sheets back into her file. 'Can I stop you?' Her eyes flicked to the two grey-suited men standing a respectful distance away in the otherwise deserted foyer. Bodyguards, she supposed. 'I imagine Tweedle Dum and Tweedle Dee make it their business to see you get what you want.'

'Georg and Karl.'

'You give them names?'

His mouth quirked into a smile. 'Actually, no. In Andovaria we still consider the naming of children to be entirely the prerogative of the respective parents.'

He sat beside her as blithely as if the last ten years hadn't happened. 'Unlike Denmark, where the queen needs to give permission for the use of any name not on the approved list.'

'How forward-thinking of you.'

'We like to think so.'

Marianne gave her head a little shake as though it would somehow bring the planets back into alignment. He said the name of his country as easily as if he'd never lied to her. He seemed to take it for granted she'd know it now and there was nothing to be gained by pretending she didn't.

His photograph was beamed all over the world. Every hairdresser in the country probably had a magazine with his picture in it. She'd seen him skiing, mountain walking, standing on the steps of Poltenbrunn Castle, at assorted royal weddings…including his own.

She even remembered the name of the girl he'd married—and divorced, although they'd called it an annulment. Amelie. Amelie of Saxe-Broden. Everything about that wedding seemed to have attracted the attention of the world's media and she'd not been able to shut it out.

If she'd needed any other impetus to get on with her life, that had been it.

Marianne drew a deep breath. 'So, what brings you to England? Is there some royal event I missed hearing about?'

He shook his head. 'No, this is an entirely private visit.'

'How lovely.' The sarcastic edge to her voice shocked her. *What was happening?* She felt like a piece of fabric that had started to fray. Marianne bent to put her file into her briefcase as sudden hot tears—part anger, part sadness—stung the back of her eyes.

She *mustn't cry. Damn it!* She'd done more than enough of that. It was as though seeing him again had pierced a hole in the dam she'd built to protect her from all the emotions of that time.

Marianne pulled her briefcase onto her knee and concentrated on fastening the clasp. 'Are you travelling incognito this time?' She spared him a glance. 'I suppose the men in grey,' she said, looking at Georg and Karl, 'might curb the possibilities a bit.'

Seb's already dark eyes took on a deeper hue. 'You're still angry with me.'

Something inside her snapped. 'Just what exactly did you think I'd be?'

'I suppose…' Seb twisted the ring on his right hand and glanced over his shoulder as though to make sure the foyer was still empty of anyone who might be listening. 'I suppose I hoped—'

'You hoped. What? That I'd somehow have forgotten you walked off into the night and didn't bother to contact me? Th-that you lied to me?

Funnily enough, Seb, that kind of thing tends to stay with you.'

'I—'

She cut him off. 'Lovely though this has been, I'm afraid I've got to go. I've got an incredibly busy morning and—' she stood up and Seb stood with her '—I need to gather my thoughts.'

'Marianne, I—'

'Don't!' She adjusted her grip on the handle of her briefcase. 'D-don't you dare. It's a full decade since I've been remotely interested in anything you have to say.'

'I didn't lie to you.'

About to walk away, Marianne froze. *How dared he?* How *dared* he stand there and say that—to *her?* For a moment she was too dumbfounded to answer.

Then, on a burst of anger, 'Really? Somehow I must have misheard you telling me you were Andovarian royalty. How can I have got it that muddled? Stupid, stupid me!'

His face reacted as though she'd slapped him. Strangely that didn't feel as fantastic as she'd thought it would, but she continued relentlessly,

'And to think I've just spent years of my life thinking what a complete waster you are.'

Seb stood a little straighter. 'I admit I didn't tell you I was the crown prince—'

'No, you didn't!'

'—but there were reasons for that.'

Marianne almost snorted with contempt. It hadn't taken much introspection, even at eighteen, for her to work that out for herself. Faced with the discovery *her* Seb Rodier was about to be enthroned as his country's ruler, she'd made a good guess at what those reasons might be.

Only she didn't share his belief they were justifiable. Ever. No one had the right to treat someone as he had her. Crown prince or not.

'Rodier is my family name. I didn't lie to you about that and I—'

'Of course, that makes all the difference,' she said silkily, still keeping her voice low. 'You knew I'd no idea who you were and you deliberately omitted telling me. I didn't even know you weren't Austrian. I'd never even heard of Andovaria. *You* certainly never mentioned it and I dare say you made sure Nick didn't either.'

'I never told you I was Austrian.'

'You said you lived a short drive from Vienna.'

'Which is true. I…'

Marianne closed her eyes. This was a childish and pointless conversation—and she'd reached the end of what she could cope with. She held up her free hand as though it had the power to ward off anything else he might say. 'Honestly, I don't care any more if your real name is Ambrose Bucket and you live in the vicinity of Saturn. It wouldn't change anything. You *did* lie to me— and I *don't* forgive you.' She would *never* forgive him as long as she had breath in her body.

'Marianne—'

'No!' *No more*. Her one coherent thought was that she needed to escape. Anywhere—as long as it put enough distance between herself and His Serene *bloody* Highness.

She kept her back straight and one foot moving in front of the other. She needed air and she needed it now. Marianne headed straight for the wide double doors and practically ran down the shallow steps.

Seb. Seb Rodier. Even though she knew he was the ruling prince of a wealthy alpine principality she couldn't think of him that way. To her this

Seb was merely an older version of the nineteen-year-old language student she'd met in Amiens. The one she'd eaten crêpes with, walked beside the River Seine with and, *damn it,* loved.

Marianne bit down so hard on her bottom lip she drew blood. *Oh, God.* Not swearing, praying. She just wanted the memories to stop flooding through her.

Her feet slowed because they had no choice. London traffic blocked her way and the coffee shop she wanted was on the other side of the road.

And *why* was she running anyway? Experience had taught her that there was nowhere to go that would stop the pain from jogging alongside. More slowly she crossed the road, dodging between the stationary taxis that were banked up at the junction.

Coffee. That was all she wanted right now. Coffee and a moment to gather herself together. She smiled grimly. Just enough time to place the mask firmly back in place.

Seb let out his breath in one slow, steady stream, resisting the temptation to swear long and hard, as he watched Marianne walk away.

That could have gone better. It had been a long, long time since anyone had made him look, or feel, quite so foolish. How many sentences had he managed to complete at the end there? Two? Maybe three?

For a man who was famed for his ability to say the right thing in any social situation, that was unprecedented. As unprecedented as it was for anyone to speak to him without the due deference his position demanded. Thank heaven the foyer was deserted of everyone but his own people.

Seb looked over his shoulder at his two body-guards. 'How much of that did you hear?'

He saw Karl's lips twitch. In any other man the expression would have counted as impassive, but in Karl it was laughter.

Seb ran an exasperated hand through his closely cropped dark hair. 'Try and forget it,' he said, walking past them and further into the narrow reception area.

It was an unnecessary instruction. Karl and Georg would never divulge anything about his personal life—not to the Press, not even to other members of their team. He'd do better to direct that selfsame instruction at himself—try and forget it. Concentrate on what had brought him here.

But forget *her*?

He pulled a wry smile. Now, that was easier said than done. If merely reading the name Marianne Chambers in print had pulled him up short, it was nothing compared to how it had felt to actually see her.

Until that moment he hadn't truly believed Professor Blackwell's protégée would turn out to be the language student he'd met in France—but she'd been instantly recognisable. Casually dressed in blue jeans and white T-shirt she'd reminded him so much of the eighteen-year-old he'd known. He could never have expected that.

And she'd been reading. Something had snapped inside him when he'd seen the flash of white as she'd flicked over the page. She'd always been reading. Anything and everything. Even that first time—when Nick had tried so hard to stop him going to speak to her.

It was the only excuse he'd had for approaching her. If there'd been anyone within earshot… Seb pulled a hand through his hair. God only knew what the headlines would have looked like then.

'Your Serene Highness—'

Seb turned to see an agitated man scurrying towards him across the acres of rather dated carpet in the company of his private secretary.

'—we'd no idea you'd arrived yet. I'd intended to have someone on watch for you and—'

'It's of no consequence. Mr…?'

'Baverstock. Anthony Baverstock. I'm the manager here, Your Serene Highness.'

'Baverstock,' Seb repeated, extending his hand. 'I sincerely appreciate the thought.' He watched the pleased way Anthony Baverstock puffed out his cheeks and resigned himself to what experience had taught him would follow.

'N-not at all, Your Serene Highness. At the Cowper Hotel we pride ourselves on our service. Professor Blackwell,' the hotel manager continued with every indication that he would bore his friends and neighbours with his account of meeting royalty for the next thirty years, 'is in the Balcony Room. If, Your Serene Highness, would be so good as to follow me…'

Seb let his mind wander even while his mouth said everything that his late father would have wished. How many times had that amazing man cautioned him to remember that people who met him would remember the occasion as long as they lived?

It was true, too. The letters of condolence his mother had received had been testament to that. More than several hundred had begun with 'I met Prince Franz-Josef and he shook me by the hand…'

Even eight years and as many months into his own tenure that responsibility still sat uncomfortably with him. But training was everything—and this had been his destiny since the hour of his birth. Inescapable. Even though there'd been times when he'd have gladly passed the responsibility to someone else.

Viktoria, for example. His elder sister had always found her role in this colourful pageant easier to play. She loved the pomp and the sense of tradition. It suited her—and she was as comfortable with it as it chafed him.

The Balcony Room on the first floor was clearly labelled. A black plaque with gold lettering hung on the door. Seb stood back and allowed the hotel manager to announce portentously, 'His Serene Highness, the Prince of Andovaria.'

Inside, the man he'd come to see was on his feet immediately. 'Your Serene Highness…'

Seb extended his hand as he walked into the room. 'Professor Blackwell, I'm delighted you could spare me a moment of your time. I realise this is a busy time for you.'

The older man shook his head, a twinkle of pure enthusiasm lighting the eyes behind his glasses. 'Completely enjoyable. This conference is one of the highlights of my year.'

'May I introduce my private secretary, Alois von Dietrich? I believe you've spoken.'

The professor nodded. 'Please, come and sit down,' he said, indicating a group of four armchairs by the window, 'but I meant what I said yesterday. I'm retiring at the end of the month.'

Seb smiled. 'I'm here in person to tempt you away from that decision.'

'Don't believe I'm not tempted,' the professor said with a shake of his head, and his tone was so wistful that Seb was confident of success. 'The twelfth and thirteenth centuries are my particular passion. My wife would have it it's an un-healthy obsession.'

'Which is exactly why I want you to come to Andovaria.'

Marianne sat down in the nearest armchair and tucked her hair behind her ears in the nervous gesture she'd had since childhood.

'Why didn't you tell me?'

Professor Blackwell shook his head. 'I've scarcely had a chance,' he said, sitting opposite her, teacup in hand. 'I spoke to one of his aides late yesterday afternoon and Prince Sebastian in person this morning.

She frowned. 'And you're considering it? Going to Andovaria?'

'Who wouldn't?' The professor picked up the shortbread biscuit resting in his saucer. 'I know what you're thinking, Marianne, and you're right. Of course you're right. But it's the chance of a lifetime. If the prince's description is accurate, and there's no reason to suppose it isn't, there's not been anything like it in decades.'

Marianne sat in silence, more than a little

shell-shocked, while the professor drank the last of his tea.

'Imagine for a moment what we might find there,' he said, standing up and putting his cup and saucer back on the table.

'You're weeks from retiring,' she said softly. 'You did tell him that, didn't you?'

'Eliana will understand—'

'She won't, Peter. You and I both know that if your wife had had her way you'd be retired now.'

The professor sat down again and leant forward to take hold of her hands. 'This is the "big" one, Marianne. I've waited my whole life for something like this.'

His earnest, lined face shone with the absolute certainty she'd understand, and the tragedy was, she did. Marianne understood absolutely how much he'd want this—and how completely impossible it was for him to take it.

'Have you told him about your eyesight?' she asked gently.

The professor let go of her hands and sat back in his seat.

She hated to do this to him, hated it particularly because he was the most wonderful, brilliant and caring man she'd ever met, but it was an impossible dream. He had to know that—deep down. 'You can't see well enough to do this justice and, if it's as significant as you think it is, you ought to pass it on to another expert. I can think of upward of a dozen who are eminently qualified, half a dozen I'd be happy with.'

He shook his head. 'We could do it together. I've told him I'd need to bring a colleague—'

'I'm too junior,' Marianne objected firmly. 'I've got years of study ahead of me before I'd be ready to take on something like this.'

'You could be my eyes. You've a sharp, analytical mind and we're a great team.' The professor stood up abruptly and brushed the crumbs off his tie. 'Let's not discuss it any more until after dinner tonight. There's plenty of time before I have to give him my final decision.'

After what dinner? Her mind went into spasm and the question in her head didn't make words as the professor adjusted his reactor light glasses and continued, 'You and I can talk about it after we've seen the photographs. There is a stack of them apparently and I'll need you there to take a look at them.'

'Wh-what dinner?'

'Didn't I say?' His assumed nonchalance would have been comical if the stakes weren't so high. 'Prince Sebastian has invited us to dinner at the Randall. At eight,' he added as Marianne still hadn't spoken.

Her mind was thinking in short bursts. *Dinner with Sebastian. Tonight. At Eight.*

'Us?'

'Of course, us.' The professor sounded uncharacteristically tetchy. 'I told him I'd need to discuss the offer with my colleague and he, very graciously, extended the invitation to you.'

Marianne swallowed as a new concern slid into her befuddled mind. 'You've told him you're bringing me? B-by name? He knows it'll be me?'

The professor made a tutting sound as though he couldn't understand why her conversation had become so unintelligible. 'I can't remember what I said exactly—but why should that matter? Prince Sebastian wants me, and whatever team I care to assemble. I chose you.'

At any other time his confidence in her ability would have warmed her, but...

The professor didn't understand what he was

asking—and, after ten years of keeping it a secret from him, she'd no intention of telling him now. But…

Dinner with Seb.

Who might not even know she was Professor Blackwell's colleague?

'We look at the photographs, we eat his food and then we take a taxi back here.' The Professor smiled the smile of an impish child. 'After that, we'll talk about it.'

CHAPTER TWO

THE new dress wasn't working.

Marianne stared at her reflection and at the soft folds of pink silk which draped around her curves to finish demurely in handkerchief points at her ankles. On the outside the transformation from serious academic to sophisticated lady-about-town was staggering, but on the inside, where it mattered, Marianne felt as if she was about to take a trip in a tumbrel.

What was she doing? There was no way she should have allowed Peter to talk her into this dinner. No way at all. Yet, even while every rational thought in her head had been prompting her to get herself back on the train home to Cambridge, she'd found herself in Harvey Nic's, picking out a dress.

And why? She was too honest a person not to know that on some level or other it was because she wanted Seb to take one look at her and experience a profound sense of regret.

Stupid! So stupid! What part of her brain had decreed that a bright idea? She'd squandered a good chunk of her 'kitchen fund' on a daft dress to impress a man who only had to snap his fingers to induce model-type beauties to run from all directions.

It was far, far more likely he'd take one look at her and know she'd made all this effort to impress him. And how pitiful would that look?

Marianne turned away from the mirror and walked over to the utilitarian bedside table common to all the hotel's rooms. She sat on the side of the bed and roughly pulled open the drawer, picking up the only thing inside it—a heart-shaped locket in white gold. Her hand closed round it and she took a steadying breath.

Heaven help her, she *was* going to go with Peter tonight. The decision had been made. She might as well accept that. And she was going to pretend she was fine.

More than that, she was going to pretend she'd forgotten almost everything about Seb Rodier.

He'd been a minor blip in her life. Quickly recovered from...

'Marianne?'

There was a discreet knock on the door and Marianne quickly replaced the locket, shutting the drawer and moving to pick up her coordinating handbag and fine wool wrap from the end of the bed.

The deep pink of the wrap picked out the darkest shade in the silk of her dress, while the bag exactly matched her wickedly expensive sandals. That they also pinched the little toe on her right foot would serve as an excellent reminder of her own stupidity.

'You look very lovely,' the professor said by way of greeting. 'Not that you don't always, but I spoke to Eliana just over half an hour ago and she was worried you wouldn't have brought anything with you that would be suitable for dinner at the Randall. I said I was sure you'd manage something.'

Marianne gave a half-smile and wondered how it was possible that a fearsomely intelligent man like the professor, who'd been happily married for forty-one years, could believe she'd have a dress like this rolled up in her suitcase 'just in case'.

'I'm excited about this dinner,' he said, completely oblivious to her mood. 'Of course, what the prince is asking would mean I'd have to give up all of the projects I'm currently involved with.'

She reached out and pressed the lift button. 'You're retiring, Peter. You're supposed to be taking the opportunity to spend more time with your grandchildren…'

The professor shot her a smile and pulled out a folded piece of paper from the pocket of his dinner jacket. 'I spoke to one of Prince Sebastian's aides this afternoon about what's expected of us tonight with regard to royal protocol and the like. It all seems fairly straightforward,' he said, passing across the sheet. 'Apparently the prince is not one to stand on too much ceremony, thank God.'

A cold sensation washed over Marianne as she unfolded the paper. This was an aspect of the evening ahead of her she hadn't considered. If Seb thought she was going to curtsey he could go take a running jump.

'I think I've got it straight in my mind,' the professor continued, reaching out to hold the bar as the lift juddered to a stop. 'When we first meet him we address him as 'Your Serene Highness', but after that we can use a simple "sir".'

Marianne's eyes widened slightly. *Sir? Call Seb 'sir'?* How *exactly* did you look a man you'd slept with in the eye and call him 'sir'? Particularly when you wanted to call him a million other things that would probably have you arrested?

The doors swung open and the professor continued, 'Jolly good thing, too. Can you imagine how ridiculous it would be to have to say "Your Serene Highness" all evening? Such a mouthful.'

Her eyes skimmed the first couple of points.

—Wait for the prince to extend his hand in greeting.
—Don't initiate conversation, but wait for the prince to do so.

'It must irritate the heck out of him to have people spouting his title at him every time he steps out of doors.' The professor broke off to hail a passing black taxi. 'Not to mention having everyone you meet bob up and down in front of you like some kind of manic toy.'

Marianne's eyes searched for the word *'curtsey'*. 'Sir' she could just about cope with—

particularly if she said it in a faintly mocking tone—but curtseying to him? He'd humiliated her in practically every way possible, but that would be too much to cope with. There had to be a way round it.

Hadn't she read something somewhere about Americans not having to curtsey when they met British royalty? Something about it not being their monarch that made it an unnecessary mark of respect?

The taxi swung towards the kerb.

'And an inclination of the head when I meet him is all that's required. No need for a more formal bow,' the professor continued. 'Obviously removing any hat—'

Marianne watched as he struggled with the door before holding it open for her '—but, as I'm not wearing a hat, that's not a problem.'

She gathered up the soft folds of her dress so that it wouldn't brush along the edge of the car and climbed inside. Seb wasn't *her* monarch. If he wasn't her monarch, she didn't need to curtsey…

Moments later the professor joined her. 'Of course, as a woman, you give a slight curtsey. Nothing too flourishing. Keep it simple.'

Keep it simple. The words echoed in her head. There was nothing about this situation that was simple. She was in a taxi heading towards a former lover who may or may not know she was joining him for dinner tonight. A former lover, mark you, who hadn't had the courtesy to formally end their relationship.

'Blasted seat belts,' the professor said, trying to fasten it across him. 'They make the things so darn fiddly.'

Marianne blinked hard against the prickle of tears. She wasn't sure whether they were for her and her own frustration, or for the professor and his.

The one thing she was certain of was that they shouldn't be here. Why couldn't Peter see how pointless it was? He shouldn't even be entertaining the idea of going to Andovaria. Even a simple task like fastening a seat belt was difficult for him now.

'Done it,' the professor said, sitting back in his seat more comfortably.

She turned away and looked out of the window. *Age-related macular degeneration.* It had come on so suddenly, beginning with a slight blurriness and ending with no central vision at all. Sooner or later people would notice Peter couldn't proofread his own material.

And if he couldn't cope with something in a clear typeface, how did he imagine he was going to do justice to something written in archaic German and eight hundred years old? He'd miss something vital—and the academic world he loved so much would swoop in for the kill.

It was all such a complete mess.

Familiar landmarks whizzed past as the driver unerringly took them down side-roads and round a complicated one-way system.

The taxi slowed and pulled to a stop. 'Here we are. The Randall.'

Marianne looked up at one of London's most prestigious hotels and felt…intimidated.

All she had to do was look at the photographs, eat and leave. She could do that.

Of course she could do that. This was a business meeting. There was nothing personal about it.

Marianne's eyes followed the tier upon tier of windows, familiar from the countless postcards produced for tourists.

And this was where Seb, the real Seb, stayed

when he was in London. In France they'd booked a room in whatever inexpensive *chambre d'hôte* they'd happened upon and sat on grass verges to eat warm baguettes they'd bought from the local *boulangerie.* So different.

'That'll be £16.70, love,' the driver said, turning in his seat to look through the connecting glass.

Marianne jerked round and her fingers fumbled for the zip of her purse. 'P-please keep the change,' she said, pulling out a twenty-pound note.

It was only later, when she'd carefully tucked away the receipt in the side-pocket of her handbag and was standing on the pavement, that it occurred to her she should have let Peter settle the fare himself. She was so used to stepping in to do the tasks she knew he found difficult that it hadn't occurred to her that she ought to let him fail this time. Perhaps that might have shown him how impossible a proposition this was?

'This is something, isn't it?' the professor said gleefully, gesturing towards sleek BMWs that were so perfectly black they looked as if they'd been dipped in ink.

Marianne managed a smile as men in distinctive livery opened every door between the pavement and the imposing entrance hall. From there on it got worse. Enormous chandeliers hung from the high ceilings and gilt bronze garlands twisted their way along endless cream walls. It was the kind of awe-inspiring space that made you want to speak in hushed whispers.

'Professor Blackwell and Dr Chambers to see His Serene Highness the Prince of Andovaria,' the professor said, pulling out a simple white card on which Seb had written something. 'In the Oakland Suite.'

Marianne half expected the slightly superior young man to raise his eyebrows in disbelief. Her dress, which had seemed so expensive just an hour ago, now didn't seem quite expensive enough. She lifted her chin in determination not to be cowed by her surroundings. She'd enough of an ordeal ahead of her without falling apart simply by stepping through the door.

'Of course, sir. This way.'

More chandeliers. More bronze garlands twisting their way up and onwards. Marianne wasn't sure which way to look first. The cream walls were punctuated with huge gilt mirrors and original oil paintings, while the fresh roses arranged on each of the antique tables looked so soft and so perfect they could have been made of velvet.

She felt…overwhelmed. By pretty much everything. Even the lift moved as though it were floating. The doors opened and they stepped out into a space no less opulent than the one below. Marianne could feel her stomach churning as though a billion angry ants had been let loose.

Seb. His name thumped inside her brain. She had to keep focusing on the fact that this man wasn't Seb. Not her Seb. He was His Serene Highness the sovereign prince of Andovaria. He had nothing, absolutely *nothing* to do with her.

After the briefest of knocks the door to the Oakland Suite swung open and they were ushered, past the bodyguards, into what was rather like a mini-apartment. And it seemed that it had its own hotel staff member to take care of it because they were passed into the care of another uniformed man, who took her wrap.

Marianne felt disorientated and more cowed with every second that passed. Her chest felt tight and her breath seemed as though it were catching on cobwebs.

'This way. His Serene Highness is expecting you.'

Double doors opened onto a tastefully furnished sitting room. Three sets of glass doors lined one wall, each framed by heavy curtains complete with swags and tails, while to the far end there was a baby grand piano.

'Isn't this incredible?' the professor said as soon as they were alone. He walked over to the glass doors, which had been flung open to make the most of the warm weather, and peered out. 'There's even some kind of terrace out here. Just incredible. Come and have a look.'

But Marianne couldn't move. She knew with absolute certainty that if she tried to walk anywhere her knees would buckle under her. Never, in her entire life, had she felt so…scared. But not just scared. She was also confused, angry and hurting.

There was the muffled sound of voices and the soft click that indicated a door had shut.

Seb? Her eyes stayed riveted on the connecting doorway.

Any moment…

Drawing on reserves she didn't know she had, Marianne consciously relaxed her shoulders and lifted her chin. Seb mustn't see how completely overwrought she was by this whole experience.

The door opened and it crossed her mind to wonder whether she was about to faint for the first time in her life.

'Professor Blackwell,' Seb said, walking forward, hand outstretched. 'I'm delighted you could join me this evening.'

She'd never seen Seb in a dinner jacket. At least, not outside of a photograph. It was an inconsequential thought—and one she ought to be ashamed of—but nothing she'd seen in the various magazines had prepared her for the effect it was having on her.

Pure sex appeal.

Several years' experience of various university dinners had left her wondering why men bothered, particularly if they went for ruffles and an over-tight cummerbund. But Seb just looked sexy.

Seeing him this morning had been dreadful, but this felt so much worse. This time shock wasn't protecting her from anything. She felt…raw.

Vulnerable.

And after everything she'd experienced she should have been completely immune to a playboy prince who'd simply decided, long ago, he didn't want her any more.

Her eyes took in every detail…because she couldn't help it. The small indentation in the centre of his chin and the faint scar above his eyebrow she knew he'd got when he was seventeen and fallen off a scooter.

And he seemed so much broader. More powerful than she remembered. Beneath his beautifully cut black jacket was a body entirely more muscled than the one she'd known so intimately. But—if she traced a finger down his left side until she reached a point two centimetres above his hip bone she would find the small oval-shaped birthmark she'd kissed….

Marianne felt a tight pain in her chest and realised she needed to let go of the air she was holding in her lungs.

This was a mistake. She wasn't strong enough to do this. She saw the professor's slight nod of the head and heard the murmured, 'Your Serene Highness, may I introduce my colleague—'

Any moment Seb would look at her. Please,

God. Marianne clutched her handbag close to her body and prayed the ground would open up and swallow her whole.

'—Dr Marianne Chambers?'

Then his dark brown eyes met hers. He had beautiful, sexy eyes. Brown with flecks of deepest orange fanning out from dark black pupils.

'Your Serene Highness.' She heard her voice. Just. It was more of a croak.

But she didn't curtsey. Not so much a conscious act of defiance as the consequence of complete paralysis. She needed to tap into some of the hate she felt for him. Remember what he'd done to her. How much he'd hurt her.

'Dr Chambers.' He extended his hand and Marianne recovered enough composure to stretch out her own. 'I understand from Professor Blackwell that you're particularly knowledgeable about the Third Crusade.'

'Y-yes.' She felt his fingers close round her hand. Warm. Confident. A man in charge. 'Yes, I am.'

'Thank you for giving up your evening at such short notice.'

Seb released her hand and turned back to the professor.

Strangers. They were meeting like strangers. Everything inside of her rebelled at that. They *weren't* strangers. She wanted to scream that at him. Shout loudly. Make herself heard.

'May I introduce Dr Max Liebnitz,' Seb said smoothly, 'the curator of the Princess Elizabeth Museum?'

Marianne had barely noticed the unassuming man standing quietly behind. He moved now and shook the professor's hand. 'Delighted to meet you,' he said in heavily accented English. 'And you, Dr Chambers. I believe I may have read something of yours on the *battle of Hattin?*'

'That's possible,' Marianne murmured, conscious that Seb was standing no more than two metres away from her and could hear everything she said and everything said to her.

It was such a surreal experience. And the temptation to look at him again was immense, but she resolutely kept her focus on the professor, who'd fallen into an easy German. Her own grasp of the spoken language was less well-developed, but she knew enough to contribute to their discussion and more than enough to know Professor Blackwell had discovered a kindred spirit in Dr Leibnitz.

Seb's well-informed observations astounded her. Once, when he referred to the siege of Acre, she was surprised into looking up at him.

He'd changed. The Seb she'd known couldn't have made a comment like that. He'd been... reckless. Irresponsible. Ready for adventure. Simply younger, she supposed with a wry smile.

She tended to forget how very young she'd been herself—and how foolishly idealistic. She'd honestly believed she'd discovered her soul mate, the man she'd spend the rest of her life with, grow old with, have children with.

How foolish was that at eighteen? Marianne lifted her chin and straightened her spine. She'd paid a heavy price for her naivety, whereas Seb had recognised their relationship for what it was and survived it unscathed.

That hurt. To know that she was the only one nursing any kind of regret.

'Marianne's recent research has been particularly focused on the role of women.' The professor turned to smile at her. 'Obviously the vast bulk of primary sources available to us have been written by men—'

'And for men,' Marianne interjected, bringing her mind back into sharp focus.

Dr Leibnitz nodded. 'It must make your research particularly painstaking.'

'But fascinating,' Marianne agreed. 'Wars have always impacted on women and the Third Crusade was no different.'

Seb stood back and listened. He wasn't sure what had surprised him most—that Marianne was fluent in German or that she was so clearly respected for her opinions. Ten years ago she'd intended to pursue an English degree. So, what had made her change direction?

And the German? It was impossible not to remember the times he'd tried to instruct her in his native tongue for no other reason than he'd loved to hear the strong English accent in her appalling pronunciation. There was no trace of that any more.

Very little trace of the girl at all. This morning he'd been struck by the similarities, but this evening her ash blonde hair was swept up in a sophisticated style and her body was much more curvaceous than the image of her he held in his memory.

Still beautiful. Undeniably. Maybe more so.

And nervous. Seb wasn't sure how he knew that, but he did. There was nothing about the way Marianne was speaking that told him that. Outwardly she seemed to be a woman in control of her destiny, comfortable wherever she found herself, but…there was something. Perhaps the grip on her handbag was a little too tight? Or her back a little too straight?

She hadn't wanted to talk to him this morning— and he'd lay money on the fact she didn't want to be here tonight. He watched the soft swing of her long earrings against the fine column of her throat and he experienced a wave of…

He wasn't sure of what. Regret that he'd hurt her? Maybe that was the ache inside of him? He'd never intended to hurt her. But then he hadn't intended to do anything more than speak to her on that first day. Not much more than that on the second.

They had all four of them been travelling through France. What was more sensible than that he and Nick should join forces with Marianne and Beth? At least, that was what he'd told his friend.

He'd been such a fool. He'd had no idea of the

possible consequences. But Nick had. Seb thought of his old school friend with a familiar appreciation. Nick had tried hard to persuade him to stay longer in Amiens. Had been a constant voice in his ear reminding him of what his parents would say…

Marianne's accusation this morning that he'd lied to her had startled him—and yet the more he thought about it the more ashamed he felt.

He owed her an explanation. What he lacked was the opportunity to give it. Professor Blackwell and Dr Leibnitz might be deep in conversation, but it was pushing the bounds of possibility to imagine they wouldn't be aware of what was being said in another part of the room.

Seb nodded towards the butler, who opened the double doors into the intimate dining room. The party moved through and with great skill, he thought, he encouraged the professor and Dr Leibnitz to continue their conversation uninterrupted—and that left him next to Marianne.

The butler positioned her chair behind her and she'd no choice but to accept the place. Instinct told him that she would not have if there'd been any alternative. He watched her, surreptitiously, noticing the small curl of baby-fine blonde hair that had escaped the elegant twist and had settled at the nape of her neck.

She was a very beautiful woman. And not married. She wore no rings on her left hand. In fact, she wore no jewellery—except the long, tapering earrings that swung against her neck when she spoke.

'Your German is excellent, Dr Chambers,' Seb said, forcing her to look at him.

Her eyes turned to him, startled, and the long earrings swung softly. 'Th-thank you.'

'Where did you learn it?'

The butler stepped forward and moved to fill her wine glass.

'No. Thank you. I'd prefer water.'

Seb watched the nervous flutter of her hands. 'Your German,' he persisted, 'where did you learn it? Your pronunciation is perfect.'

He saw the slight widening of her eyes and knew she was remembering the afternoon they'd spent at Monet's garden at Giverny.

She turned her head away and her earrings swung. Marianne didn't seem to notice the way they brushed her neck. 'Eliana…' She swallowed. 'Eliana, Professor Blackwell's wife, is Austrian. From Salzburg.'

Seb frowned his confusion. He didn't immediately see the connection…

'I lived with Professor Blackwell and his family when I…was younger.'

He could have sworn she'd been about to say something different. His mind played through the options. When I…finished university? When I…started work? *When I…came back from Paris?*

He wanted to know. Certainly Marianne hadn't lived with the professor's family before France. She'd lived with her parents in a village in…Suffolk.

'Eliana and Peter are close family friends of my father's sister.'

Ah. Seb's eyes flicked across to the professor, still firmly engrossed in his conversation on the finer points of twelfth-century sword design. 'And is that why you chose to study history?'

Again her soft brown eyes turned on him with a startled expression. She gave the slightest of smiles. 'His enthusiasm is infectious.'

No doubt that was true, but Seb felt that her answer was only half the story. Ten years ago she'd had ambitions to write plays that would rival Shakespeare. She'd set herself the goal of reading her way through the entire works of Chekhov and Ibsen by the time she started university. So, what had changed?

'I imagine it is. Professor Blackwell's reputation is second to none.' Seb paused while the butler placed the beautifully presented foie gras and wild-mushroom bourdin in front of him. 'That's why my sister is adamant I must persuade him to come to Andovaria.'

'Your sister?'

'Viktoria. My eldest sister. The Princess Elizabeth Museum is in my grandmother's memory and Vik's pet project.'

Marianne's mind felt as if it was spluttering. 'Vik' would be Her Serene Highness, Princess Viktoria? Tall, elegant, married to some equally tall and well-connected title with two young sons?

She looked down at the heavily starched table-cloth, bedecked with more cutlery choices than she'd ever faced in her life, and tried to focus on what had brought her here. 'But if much of what you have beneath the palace is connected with the Teutonic knights, then surely Professor Adler would be the obvious choice?'

Seb picked up his wine glass and took a sip. 'That's true, but we believe only a small part of what we have would be of particular interest to Professor Adler.'

The first course gave way to the second. And after the breast of guinea-fowl with asparagus and bacon came the third, an artistic arrangement of dark chocolate with a praline ice cream.

Marianne took a tiny spoonful of the ice cream. Somehow Seb managed to make it sound so *reasonable* that the professor should go to Andovaria and, if it weren't for his eyesight, he *was* the perfect choice.

Her eyes flicked to the animated, kindly face of the professor opposite. Excitement was practically radiating from him. It was a tangible thing.

He wouldn't be able to resist this opportunity. Marianne knew it with complete certainty. A lifetime devoted to uncovering the secrets of the past couldn't be pushed to one side easily.

And she couldn't, *wouldn't*, leave him to flounder alone. As much as she hated the thought of going to Andovaria, she loved Peter and

Eliana more. She owed them something for what they'd done for her.

More than something. Marianne took a sip of water. They'd taken her in, pregnant and scared, when her own mother had not. She owed them everything. She took another mouthful of ice cream and let her eyes wander to Seb's handsome profile. Supremely confident, charismatic and charming. He really had no idea of the fate he'd left her to.

What would Seb say if he knew he'd left her expecting their baby?

Had he ever thought to wonder what had happened to her? Or had he really returned to Andovaria and his royal responsibilities without sparing her a moment's consideration?

What kind of conversation would they be having now if little Jessica had lived?

In many ways nature had known best. It hurt her to think it, but at eighteen she'd been hopelessly ill-prepared to take on the responsibility of a child. The logical part of her brain accepted that, even while her heart probably never would. Eliana had spent hours talking her through…everything. Patiently helping her manage emotions she'd not had the life skills to even begin to deal with.

First, there'd been the pregnancy itself and her mother's inability to cope with her 'perfect' daughter's fall from grace.

And then the stillbirth. The heartbreaking scan. The long hours of labour which had resulted in a perfectly formed baby girl—born asleep, as the euphemism went.

Marianne covertly studied His Serene Highness Prince Sebastian II. *Their* baby. She and Seb had created a little girl—and he didn't even know.

She reached out for her water glass and took a sip, carefully placing it back down on the table. Eliana believed all men had the right to know if they were about to become a father…

Sometimes she wondered…if Jessica had lived long enough to be born safely, whether she'd ever have told him. At eighteen she'd been adamant he'd never know, but that had been her hurt talking. The first photographs of the about-to-be-enthroned Prince of Andovaria with his dark-haired fiancée had been cataclysmic. Like a switch flicking inside her—love to hate in a moment.

She sat back in her chair. But…eventually she might have told him. Perhaps. When Jessica had grown old enough to decide whether she wanted the poisoned chalice of being universally known as the illegitimate daughter of a European prince—with a mother he'd not considered worth marrying.

It was an academic question. There'd been no baby past the seventh month of her pregnancy. Marianne could feel the pain now, shooting through her—as it always did whenever she was reminded of Jessica. The sense of failure. And the emptiness that pervaded everything—and had done for practically her entire adult life.

She watched as Seb reached for his wine glass. He'd no idea. No understanding of how comprehensively he'd wrecked her life. And how she'd *never* forgive him.

CHAPTER THREE

THE photographs were fascinating. Far more so than Marianne had expected.

'This is quite remarkable. Remarkable,' the professor mumbled. 'Everything completely shut away…'

'Yes,' Seb agreed, moving to stand behind him. 'Until the renovation work began on that part of the castle, no one alive knew the rooms were even there.'

Marianne's eyes instinctively followed Seb as he walked across the room, helplessly noticing the way his jacket skimmed the powerful shoulders of a man she knew had become an Olympic skier.

It was peculiar to think that she knew so much about him, whereas he knew nothing about her since he'd left her in Paris. She forced herself to look back down at the 10" x 8" photograph of a long, narrow room with row upon row of serviceable shelving filled to capacity.

'Is nothing in here catalogued?' the professor asked, pointing at the image he was holding.

'No.'

Dr Leibnitz nodded his agreement. 'So far, all we've done is make a very cursory inventory. There's been no attempt at any sort of organisation.'

'Marianne?' The professor's voice startled her. 'What do you think?'

What did she think? Marianne looked up. 'I think it's a mammoth responsibility,' she said carefully.

He nodded. 'This needs a team.'

Seb sat down in an elegant Queen Anne armchair, his attention fixed on the professor. 'What we're hoping is you'll feel able to head up that team. Handpick the people you want to work with you.'

'Why me?'

'Because you're highly respected in your field,' Seb answered, his voice deep, sexy and tugging at all kinds of memories she didn't want to remember. Certainly not now. Not with Seb sitting so close to her. Marianne swallowed the hard lump that appeared to be wedged in her throat and deliberately looked down at the photograph in her hand.

'As are many others.'

Marianne's eyes skittered away from it as Seb leant forward on his chair. She looked back down, silently cursing. Somehow she needed to bring herself under a tighter control. Every movement he made, every blasted thing he did, she seemed to notice.

'Andovaria is a small principality. Bigger than Liechtenstein or Monaco, but nowhere near the size of Austria or Switzerland. The sheer quantity of what we've found has made us think much of it might not rightly belong in Andovaria.'

'And you have a problem with that?' the professor asked quickly.

'Not at all.'

Marianne caught the edge of Seb's smile in her peripheral vision and she felt her breath catch. For years she'd wondered why she'd talked Beth into letting the boys join them—and now she knew.

'My sister's adamant that everything is kept in the way that will best preserve it for future generations.' Seb paused. 'But my primary responsibility is to Andovaria and I intend to ensure that everything that rightfully belongs to my country stays within our boundaries.'

He stood up and Marianne noticed the powerful clench of his thigh muscle. 'And the easiest way, by far, is to put someone in charge of the project who has a neutral interest in what's found.'

'My interest is far from neutral.'

Seb smiled again and the pain in her chest intensified.

'But you're not actively seeking government funding or trying to raise the profile of any one particular museum....' Seb's words hung in the air.

The odds had always been weighted in favour of going to Andovaria, Marianne knew, but now it felt like a foregone conclusion. Peter would most definitely accept. How could he not? And how could she argue against it when it was clear his eyes wouldn't be the ones evaluating every single piece, or writing every report?

Damn it!

Marianne put the photograph back down on the table. A sharp pain burst in her temple and shot down the left side of her neck. She raised a shaky hand and rubbed gently across her forehead.

Could she honestly go to Andovaria with Peter?

Maybe this was fate's way of giving her that much talked-of 'closure'? Maybe spending time in Seb's country was exactly what she needed? And all it required was courage?

Her fingers moved in concentric circles against the pain in her temple. She was aware of Dr Leibnitz speculating about what might be found beneath Poltenbrunn Castle and the professor's comments about the Habsburg dynasty and Rudolf von der Hapichtsburg in particular.

'Marianne, are you feeling all right?' the professor asked, breaking off his conversation.

Her hand stilled and she forced a smile. 'I've a slight headache. It's nothing.'

'Perhaps some air?' Dr Liebnitz suggested. 'Shall I sit with you on the terrace for a moment, Dr Chambers?'

'N-no, thank you. I'm fine. It'll pass in a moment.'

Seb stood up and the abrupt movement startled her. 'I'll keep Dr Chambers company on the terrace while you continue your conversation,

Max. It's a little stuffy in here and I'd appreciate some fresh air myself.'

Panic ripped through her. 'N-no. I—'

'The terrace is very pretty,' Seb interrupted smoothly, 'with a stunning view over Green Park. Whenever I'm in London I particularly ask for this suite for that reason.'

His arm gestured towards the open glass doors and Marianne knew she had very little choice but to acquiesce with as much dignity as she could manage. 'Thank you.'

By the time she was on her feet Seb was already standing by the doors, waiting. She didn't dare look up at him as she walked out onto the terrace. A light breeze tugged at the silk of her dress, but the evening was warm enough. Almost. She gave a slight shiver, although that might have had nothing to do with the temperature outside.

'Are you cold?' he asked quickly. 'Do you have a wrap Warner could fetch for you?'

Marianne turned. 'Warner?'

'He's the butler this evening.'

'Ah.' *Warner was the butler.* She'd forgotten— the staff had names. Although Warner, it seemed, didn't warrant the use of his Christian name. So much for the equality of mankind. Marianne shook her head. 'No. Thank you.' It was nice to feel the breeze brushing against her skin. Nice to feel something other than the tight, constrained sensation in her chest.

She looked round the terrace. It was tiny, but beautifully formed—and the view was spectacular even at night. Seb was right about that. Marianne turned round and caught him watching her. His expression made her nervous and she looked away, stumbling into speech. 'Th-this is all rather…incredible,' she said, gesturing at the display of lights below them.

Seb moved closer. She could smell the light musky scent of his aftershave. *Feel* him breathing next to her.

'The terrace?' he asked quietly. 'The view? Or us being together again?'

Marianne felt her throat constrict. Her eyes turned to look at him as though she was compelled to do so. 'All of it,' she said after a moment, her voice breathy.

Silence. Then Seb smiled and it still had the ability to seduce her. *Why* was that? Other men had smiled at her with just that look in their eyes, but they'd never made her feel so light-headed.

Marianne wrapped her arms around her waist in a movement she recognised as defensive, but she didn't move away. There was a part of her that was very proud of that. 'I didn't curtsey.'

'Pardon?'

'When I arrived. I didn't curtsey to you.' For some reason it suddenly seemed so important he knew that.

A spark of laughter lit his dark eyes and he glinted down at her. 'I think we're a little past that. Certainly in private.'

'I'm not doing it in public either,' she shot back, irritated by the suspicion he was laughing at her. Marianne nervously fingered the back hook of one of her earrings. 'Did you know I was coming with the professor tonight?'

'Yes.'

She desperately wanted to ask what he'd thought about her coming. Did he find this situation as awkward as she did? But of course, that was impossible. He'd spoken to her as though they were strangers—and that was what they were. *Strangers*.

'Peter couldn't remember exactly what he'd told you. Whether I'd been a nameless colleague…'

'No.'

No. Her eyes flicked up and away again. There was some comfort in hearing that he'd invited her to join them this evening *knowing* it was her. The hum of the traffic far below filled the awkward pause. 'Oh.' And then, 'Were you surprised when he mentioned my name?'

'Very.'

She could hear something like a smile in his voice and risked another look at him. *It was a mistake*. His eyes hadn't changed. There might be fine lines fanning out at the edges now, but they were achingly familiar.

'I knew there was a slight possibility I might see you at the conference, but that Professor Blackwell would refuse to come to Andovaria without you…' His mouth twisted and he shook his head. 'No, that part surprised me. You've done exceptionally well.'

She had, but she didn't need him to tell her that. She felt as if she'd suffered the verbal equivalent of a regal pat on the head.

'He made it very clear this morning his

decision on whether he'd accept or not would be made in consultation with you. It's impressive to have achieved that level of professional respect by the age of twenty-eight.'

Seb knew how old she was. He'd remembered the fifteen-month age difference between them. Marianne swallowed—and it felt a monumentally difficult thing to do. It was as though every normal function was now something that required conscious effort.

But then, Seb was standing so close. If she stretched out her hand she could touch him… If she leant in close he could hold her… It was bound to be difficult.

'So, what do you think?'

Marianne blinked hard at the tears scratching at her eyes. 'About?'

'Coming to Andovaria? Do you have a husband to keep you in England? Family?' he added when she'd yet to answer.

'No husband.'

'Boyfriend?'

Now, that was none of his business. Marianne swivelled round and schooled her features into the expression she habitually used to quash anyone who thought to question a young blonde female's ability to have opinions that ran counter to their own. 'Andovaria is only a short flight away,' she said brusquely. 'If the professor decides to accept, I'll come with him. It's a good career opportunity for me.'

'And that's important to you?'

'Of course. It's the driving force of my life.'

There was a small beat before he asked, 'What do you think the professor's thinking?'

Marianne shook her head. 'He'll let you know when he's ready.'

'And you don't have a preference?'

His question was multi-faceted—and they both knew it. She looked down, apparently fascinated by the shades of pink that swirled together on the skirt of her dress. 'I—I didn't say that.'

'Marianne—'

Her control snapped. 'Don't!' She turned away as though to go back into the sitting room.

'We need to talk.'

'Not here,' she said in almost a whisper. 'This isn't the place.'

'It's the best we have.' And then when she didn't move away any further, 'I get the impression that Max and Professor Blackwell will hardly miss us however long we're out here.'

He saw the faint nod of her head, her earrings swinging back and forth.

'And there's no one to hear us out here.'

Marianne stood motionless for a moment as though she was deciding what to do. The breeze caught at the light fabric of her dress. And he waited, completely uncertain whether she'd turn or walk back inside.

'I suppose that's important,' she said at last, turning back to face him.

Marianne shivered again and wrapped her arms tightly around her. It hurt him to see her looking so…strained. That wasn't the way he remembered her looking at him.

'What do you want to tell me?' She rubbed at her arms.

Another shiver. 'You're cold. If we were really on our own I'd give you my jacket.'

She seemed to uncoil and a spark of anger lit her eyes. 'Well, that's just a lovely offer, Your Serene Highness.'

It took a moment for him to remember what she was remembering. *The walk in the park. The rain.*

The kiss. She'd looked so incredibly sexy in his sweatshirt, the sleeves rolled over three times…

The situation had been different then. For those brief weeks he'd been free—as he hadn't been since. That summer the embargo on reporting his private life had miraculously held. There'd been no bodyguards, no responsibilities and, amazingly, no paparazzi. He'd been free to act exactly as he wished without reference to anyone or anything.

And what he'd wanted had been Marianne.

Seb broke eye contact and crossed back to the sitting room, beckoning to the butler. 'Could you find Dr Chambers something to keep her warm?'

'Very good, sir.'

'And bring us a bottle of the dry white and a couple of glasses.'

His answer was a slight nod.

'Thank you.' He turned back to Marianne, fascinated by the pulse beating in her neck. 'Shall we sit down?'

There was a moment's hesitation before she decided to do just that. She sat herself facing out over the terrace, her eyes fixed at some point out in the distance, back straight and hands gripped in her lap.

Seb positioned himself opposite. Bizarrely, now she was sitting there, he was in no hurry to begin. What could he say that would begin to explain?

At nineteen he'd been so overwhelmed…by everything. All he'd been able to do was react to whatever was happening in that precise moment. There'd been so much to adjust to.

And somehow he'd managed to block the image of Marianne waiting for him in Paris. Convinced himself she wasn't his most urgent priority. For someone who lived his entire life trying to do the right thing by everyone, it was ironic he'd done something so spectacularly wrong.

What was it she had said? That she'd spent years of her life thinking him a 'waster' and a 'liar'?

And yet she'd never taken her story to the Press. Never sold the photographs she must have of their time together. There wasn't an editor alive who'd have failed to snap them up. Her story would have made her thousands.

But she had more dignity than that. A cool, classy lady.

'How's Nick these days?'

Her question startled him, broke into his thoughts. Seb met her eyes and saw the steely determination. She didn't want this, didn't want any part of this conversation, but she was damned if she was going to let him see it. And she'd had enough of waiting.

'Are you still in contact with him?' she prompted when he was slow to answer. 'Or was he some kind of bodyguard and you lied about that as well? He tried hard enough to keep you away from me. Was that his job?'

Seb cleared his throat, still searching for the right words. 'We're friends. Good friends. And, for what it's worth, he thought I should have told you exactly who I was—'

'Is that supposed to make me feel better?'

From the expression on her face it certainly wasn't. Seb ran a hand across his neck, easing out the tension there. 'We're still in close contact, although I see him less often since his father's death.'

'And what was *his* real name? Archduke Nikolaus?'

'Marianne…'

Her eyes widened. 'I'm sorry, am I making this difficult for you?' she asked, her rich voice distorted by sarcasm.

'As of last April Nick's the fifteenth Duke of Aylesbury.'

Marianne looked down at her fingers and concentrated on the opal colour of her nail varnish. *Nick was a duke.* Why was she surprised? *Had she honestly expected anything different?* Nick Barrington was the fifteenth Duke of Aylesbury and Seb Rodier was His Serene Highness Prince Sebastian of Andovaria. Inadvertently she must have strayed into La-La Land and nothing was as it seemed any more.

'How's Beth?' he asked, shifting in his seat.

Marianne's head came up. 'I'd love to tell you she's the Marchioness of Basingstoke, but unfortunately she isn't. You see, *we* weren't pretending. *We* were exactly what we told you we were.'

'Did she become a lawyer?'

'Y-yes. Yes, she did.'

He'd remembered. He'd remembered a single throwaway comment Beth had made on the first afternoon they'd all spent together. And somehow that made the ground shift beneath her. She didn't want to soften towards him. She wanted to keep a steel barrier between them as protection. But…

Her voice faltered. 'She's married to an anaesthetist with a baby due in a couple of months.'

'That's great.'

'She's very happy.'

The sound of footsteps brought her head round in time to see the butler walking across the rooftop courtyard with her wrap spread out over his arm. 'Your Serene Highness. Dr Chambers,' he said as he carefully placed it round her shoulders.

'Thank you,' she said awkwardly. Intellectually she knew it was his job, but she was uncomfortable with being at the receiving end of it. In her world she opened doors for herself, found the sleeves of her own coat…

Marianne looked down and pleated the tassels together. The silence was punctuated by the precise step of the butler as he crossed the terrace, returning moments later. 'Is Professor Blackwell asking for me?' she asked, looking up, hoping for an escape route.

'He's not made any comment to me, madam,' he replied, pouring the wine with easy, practised movements.

This all felt so peculiar. A balmy night in a

beautiful setting…with a man she used to be in love with.

'I'm not drinking tonight,' she said as soon as the butler was out of earshot once more. 'Alcohol's not good for a woman with a headache.'

'I suppose that depends on why she has a headache,' Seb replied, his dark eyes seeming to see so much more than she was comfortable with. Then he picked up his own glass and drank. 'You should reconsider. This is considerably better than the paint stripper we drank together in France.'

It was a shared memory—and a happy one. Marianne felt another crack in the shield. She didn't want to thaw towards him. She wanted her anger to stay at the fore… But instead she felt the first stirrings of a smile.

To hide it she picked up her glass and sipped. The chilled wine was crisp and light, with a heady scent of lemon trees. 'It's lovely.'

He smiled. 'But not as nice as our whisky?'

Something deep inside her twisted. 'No.' Nothing would ever taste as nice as the whisky they'd drunk that night. The first time she'd ever tasted whisky and the first time she'd ever made love.

'How long did you wait for me in Paris?' he asked quietly.

Marianne let her fingers curve around the glass in her hand, watching the beads of condensation. Her mind was back in the tiny bedroom they'd shared for three nights. Nothing there but a bed, a small wardrobe and the sounds of people enjoying themselves in the nearby restaurants.

'Not long,' she said, raising her eyes. 'Madame Merchand had wanted me to start earlier so I telephoned her and said I could come immediately. It seemed sensible when you didn't phone me.' She took another sip of wine.

'Were you unhappy with them?'

Marianne looked up, surprised by his question.

'I know you left early.'

He did? How? Marianne stayed watching him, her eyes wide.

His mouth twisted. 'I did contact you. Late, I admit, but Monsieur Merchand said you'd returned home weeks before.'

That was something she didn't know. Marianne felt her chest become tight. *Seb had contacted her*. Her mind felt as if it had splintered into a billion fragments. 'N-nine weeks… all but a couple of days.'

'Did you go to another family?'

His questions felt relentless—and she didn't want to answer. Marianne shook her head. 'I went home. Beth stayed in Honfleur for the full year, but I…' She trailed off. She didn't want to think about the reasons for her return home. Or what had happened when she got there.

And Seb had spoken to Monsieur Merchand. When? Why? So many questions were streaming through her brain.

'Were you homesick?'

'I—I just needed to go home,' she countered. Marianne took a deep breath and tried to regroup. The fact that Seb had eventually tried to contact her changed nothing. Nothing at all.

He'd had her address in England. He could have reached her at any time. Even when she'd gone to live with the professor and his family she hadn't been untraceable. In fact, her mother had been so desperate to know who the father of her daughter's baby was she'd happily have passed on any man's telephone number.

'Why didn't you contact me at home?'

Marianne watched the muscle pulse in his cheek before he met her eyes. Saw his unwillingness to speak and braced herself for his reply.

'I didn't want the conversation we were going to have,' he admitted, his voice more gravelly than she'd ever heard it.

He'd rung her to finish their relationship. The thought hit Marianne with a dull thud.

Seb shifted in his seat. 'I felt…grateful to have been let off the hook. The fact that you'd left France…seemed to make everything easier.'

Well, that was honest. The dispassionate part of her admired him for that even while she felt desperately hurt by what he was saying.

'I should have made more effort to speak to you.'

'It would have been nice if you'd written,' Marianne suggested in a voice that sounded small in her own ears. 'For weeks I didn't know what had happened to you. I'd no way of contacting you—'

Seb shook his head and his eyes seemed to be asking for understanding. 'I was advised against that. I was told to put nothing in writing—'

'Why?' The question was out of her mouth even as the answer flooded her mind. A frown pulled at her forehead. 'You thought I'd sell it? You...*bastard!* You pompous—'

'Marianne, they don't know you. It wasn't based on any personal evaluation—'

'You did! You knew me.' It took every ounce of control she had not to tip what was left of her wine over him. How *dared* he think that about her? 'You should have known I'd never do anything like that. I—'

'I was a coward,' Seb interrupted her. 'I should have come to England and spoken to you about what was happening in my life. If I'd been older, felt more in control of what was happening...'

He trailed off for the second time, but Marianne almost didn't notice. She was incandescently angry. It felt like a bright light burning inside her.

Everything was so much worse than she'd thought. She hadn't believed that could be possible.

But Seb had returned to Andovaria and turned their perfect, private little world into something sordid. He'd sat around with his advisers while they debated how best to 'manage' her. While she...

Dear God.

She felt hot tears prick insistently behind her eyelids and blinked furiously. She wouldn't cry. *Mustn't*. But the thought of their beautiful romance being talked over, discussed and dissected…

One single tear welled up and spilled down her cheek.

'Marianne.' Seb's voice cracked and he reached out as though to touch her.

'No!' She furiously brushed away the trail of moisture.

'I'm sorry—'

'So you say,' Marianne said, standing up abruptly. 'I think I've heard enough of your explanations now. You're sorry, I'm sorry, we're both sorry. Let's just leave it at that, shall we?'

'I haven't told you what happened when I got home. Why I—'

Marianne laughed. It wasn't a joyous sound, but hard and brittle. 'What's to understand? You forget I know practically everything about you. You're tabloid fodder. Shortly after your marriage to Amelie of Saxe-Broden, eighteen,' she said, her fingers moving to make speech marks in the air, 'you were enthroned as the Sovereign Prince of Andovaria. I've seen the pictures!'

She brushed again at another betraying tear that was making its way down her carefully made up face.

'It wasn't quite as you make that sound.'

She turned on him. 'In what way was it different, Seb?' she said in a voice laced with sarcasm. 'The Andovarian tourist industry fancied producing some memorabilia? Thought she'd look good on a stamp, perhaps?'

If he'd raised his voice or moved towards her she'd have turned and walked back into the sitting room—but he did neither. His hand rubbed at his neck and he walked over to the rail. His body language seemed to convey that she'd managed to hurt him.

Marianne felt the anger leave her like air from a balloon.

Seb didn't know anything about Jessica. However much she wanted to blame him for leaving her to deal with the consequence of their affair alone, she knew it hadn't been a conscious decision.

And she *did* want to know why he'd left her. The 'why' of it had been the thing that had prevented her from being able to truly give herself to any other relationship. The three-month cut-off, Eliana called it.

'I was called back urgently because my father was ill,' he began, his voice low and steady.

Marianne shifted her weight from one foot back to the other. 'I know.' He'd told her that at the time. She'd helped him pack. Didn't he remember?

'They'd found a tumour. In his brain.'

She knew that, too. Prince Franz-Josef's death, poignantly just weeks before his only son's marriage, had featured in glossy magazines across Europe…and probably beyond. She'd read all about it in double-page detail.

'It was inoperable and he knew he had very little time left…to make everything safe.' For the first time Seb's voice betrayed real emotion.

'Why couldn't you have rung and told me that?' she asked after a moment. 'I would have gone to Honfleur just the same and waited until—'

Seb shook his head. 'You don't understand, Marianne, it wasn't that simple.'

Why wasn't it *just* that simple? He was right. She didn't understand that. He might not have told her that he was the crown prince of Andovaria, but his identity hadn't come as a surprise to him. He'd known that when he met her. When they'd first kissed. When they'd made love…

Nothing had actually changed by his father becoming ill. Not between them.

Marianne moved closer and he must have sensed her standing there because he turned. And his eyes were…bleak. She wasn't prepared for how that would make her feel.

'God help me, I loved my father, but the months before his death were filled with far more than concern for a dying man. My life was completely turned on its head.'

'I'm sure—'

'No.' He stopped her. 'Please. Just listen.'

She nodded.

'Not just because the father I loved was dying. The Andovarian constitution…' He broke off. 'As Crown Prince, I needed to be married by my twenty-first birthday—which left me seventeen months to find a suitable bride.'

Married. To someone *suitable*. Marianne's fingers curled around the metal railing and she gripped until her knuckles showed white.

'Why…why do they have to be married?'

'Tradition.' His succinct answer came back at

her like a bullet. 'If you go back far enough all Andovarian crown princes were formally engaged before they were five or six, maybe even married in their absence.'

'How ridiculous to have something like that in the constitution,' she said, her voice husky.

'Until recently Monaco made the same requirement of their ruling prince. In the last couple of hundred years it simply hasn't been an issue in Andovaria because the crown prince has always been married by the time he succeeded.'

So why didn't you marry me? The question ricocheted around her head, even though she knew the answer. Cinderella was a fantastic fairy tale, but that was exactly what it was—a fairy tale. Crown princes didn't marry lower-middle-class girls from Suffolk. She knew it. And he knew it. In fact, he must have known it from the very beginning of their relationship.

Marianne made a conscious decision to let go of the railing in front of her. Of course he wouldn't have rushed back to Paris and demanded she marry him. That didn't happen outside romance novels and Hollywood films.

'The marriage of any member of the royal

family has to be approved by either the sovereign prince or, if he's under the age of twenty-one, by the regent. Any union entered into without it is deemed invalid and any children illegitimate.'

He said the words as though they were re-hearsed. Marianne walked slowly back towards the table and sat back down. As a historian she knew this wasn't unusual. The English constitution required the same of its royal family—and for centuries they'd duly obliged.

How did they do that, normal, flesh and blood people…with the normal, flesh and blood desire to be loved and have someone love them? How did they make themselves marry for the good of the state?

'Suddenly the question of my marriage was the number-one priority.' He hadn't moved from the railing. 'Everything was resting on me.'

In the distance Marianne could hear the hum of traffic. She wasn't really aware of anything else. In actual fact, it really wasn't so very different from what she'd always supposed had happened. She hadn't been good enough.

Not even good enough for a phone call. Not *safe* enough for a letter.

Slowly Marianne picked up her wine glass and sipped, then carefully she placed it back down in front of her.

'And…I wouldn't have been considered suitable?' She forced herself to say the words.

The slightest pause. 'No. No, you wouldn't. Weren't,' he corrected.

CHAPTER FOUR

NO. THE word echoed quietly in Marianne's head. She didn't understand why hearing Seb actually say she wasn't 'suitable' should make her feel better, but it did. Almost like a wound that had been lanced.

Years of supposition and, finally, she knew. And she'd been right all along. She was fine for a holiday romance… Fine to make love to as long as no one actually knew anything about it…

'So you married Amelie of Saxe-Broden?'

'Yes.'

'Did you love her?'

'I liked her. Still do. And I was grateful that she was prepared to take me on…but no, I didn't love her.'

Marianne swallowed hard. 'Did she know that when she married you?'

'Amelie didn't love me either. It was a

marriage that made…sense,' he said, pulling that word out with difficulty. 'We'd been brought up in the same kind of circles, but she didn't stand to inherit anything herself. She was the right age.'

His was a completely different world. Hateful, actually. He'd selected Amelie as though she'd been a brood mare.

'What would have happened if you hadn't been able to find anyone *suitable* to marry you?'

'Then I would have forfeited my right to succession and my cousin Michael would be the sovereign prince of Andovaria now.'

'I see.' Marianne shivered and pulled the wrap closely about her shoulders.

'I never intended to hurt you, Marianne. And…I'm really glad your life has turned out so well…and that…you're happy and…'

Pride was an incredibly powerful thing, she thought. Marianne forced a smile. 'You know, you could have told me the truth. Even as a little girl I never thought being a princess was much of a career plan.'

Seb's dark eyes took on a sexy glint. 'Not even when you were five?'

'I think I wanted to be an astronaut when I was five—certainly not a princess. My parents are very educationally orientated and they bought me all the books...' Seb laughed and her stomach flipped over.

'I wish I could do it differently.' He walked back to the table and sat down. 'Meeting you... becoming close to you was so unexpected. I hadn't planned any of it—'

That was true for them both, then. Falling in love with him hadn't been on her agenda either. Marianne picked up her wine glass and took another sip, determined that she would keep herself under tight control.

'—and everything happened so fast between us. There was scarcely time to think. I was in too deep to do anything about it before I'd even realised I'd begun.'

Marianne let her hands curve around the ball of her wineglass. Perhaps not the correct thing to do to a crisp white wine, but she liked the feel of the cold glass against her palm.

Their relationship had *ended* as fast as it had begun. That bothered her far more than the speed of the start. One moment she'd been little more than a child on her first big adventure, and the next she'd been yanked into adulthood.

It had been different for Seb. Meeting her hadn't altered the course of his life. After he'd left her in that Paris hotel room his world had continued on its preordained trajectory.

For her nothing had ever been the same again. If it hadn't been for her Aunt Tia contacting Eliana she wouldn't have survived. She'd have been pregnant and homeless. Her relationship with her parents fractured beyond repair.

Marianne bit her lip. What would Seb have done if he'd known they'd created a baby together? No doubt his family would have been horrified if he'd presented them with a pregnant girlfriend. They'd have probably been even more convinced of her 'unsuitability' and brokered some suitable 'arrangement' to hide his 'indiscretion'.

'There's no excuse for the way I treated you. I was young, a little rebellious, but I knew what was expected of me as the crown prince. I'd always known. I probably shouldn't even have spoken to you that first day…and I certainly shouldn't have persuaded you to let Nick and me join you.'

'Why did you?'

Why? Seb sat back in his chair and watched the way the breeze caught at the single curl on her forehead. The answer was simple—because he'd wanted to.

As simple as that.

He'd wanted to be with her.

It was probably the last occasion he'd acted without any consideration of the possible consequences. He'd wanted to talk to her…. Then he'd wanted to spend time with her…. Then…

Maybe the pivotal mistake had been going to find somewhere to buy lunch that first day. He'd been blown away by her.

And it hadn't just been her beauty that had drawn him in. He'd fallen in love with her shy smile. The way she'd blushed when he'd teased her. The way she'd laughed. Talked. Moved.

He'd never met anyone like her. That lunch had been the turning point. From that moment on everything else had been inevitable.

'I liked being with you.'

Her eyes flicked up and away again. There wasn't time to read her expression. 'Why did you agree Nick and I could join you?'

Seb watched her swallow and then search for her reply. 'I...don't know.'

'You'll have to do better than that.'

Marianne gave a slight shrug. 'Because you were so insistent? I don't know.'

There was probably more than a grain of truth in that, Seb thought. He *had* pushed hard to be allowed to join them. And Beth and Nick had followed on almost as a matter of course.

Marianne had been very young. A few weeks past her eighteenth birthday when they'd met. Innocent. And she'd made him feel important. That she seemed to like him without knowing he was a prince had done a lot for his ego too. For the first and only time in his life he'd had a taste of what it was like to be ordinary. Normal.

'Were you and Nick really on holiday?'

'Oh, yes. We'd escaped.' Seb picked up his wine and swirled it in his glass, his mind anywhere but on the liquid. 'I don't think I'd been anywhere before without some kind of protection in tow. It was a heady experience.'

'Even at school?'

'Even there. Of course, we hadn't escaped.' Seb smiled across at her. 'My parents were completely aware of where I was and what I was doing. They'd merely decided to let the leash out a little and they pulled me back in when they needed to.'

Marianne set her glass down on the table and carefully lined up the base with the edge of her coaster. 'Did they know about me?'

'I think they probably knew your shoe size.'

Had they known she was pregnant? For a moment Marianne felt quite panicked and then she calmed down. Surely her patient notes were entirely confidential. And perhaps she'd ceased to be of much interest when she'd disappeared so quietly.

From the sitting room there was the sound of laughter. Marianne looked over her shoulder. 'We shouldn't be much longer.'

'Perhaps not. How's your headache?'

'Gone. Almost.' She took a final sip of wine. Talking *had* helped. She hadn't actually learnt anything materially different from what she'd already known, but she felt…respected by his telling her. It changed nothing. And yet it changed everything.

Perhaps the most healing thing was that he

hadn't acted consciously. When she'd seen the first photographs of him with his fiancée she'd wondered whether he'd deliberately set out to have some kind of final fling. Been almost certain that he had. She looked up as a new thought burst into her head. 'You're not married now. I thought it was a requirement.' She frowned. 'Or does it all work the same way as if you were widowed?'

Seb shook his head. 'I've no heir. I needed to change the constitution.'

He changed the constitution. If it was that easy, why hadn't Seb's father changed the constitution and prevented his son being forced into a marriage he didn't want?

'It was a lengthy process, but it was necessary before Amelie and I could be granted an annulment. There hadn't been anything like it in eight hundred years of continuous rule so there were constitutional implications. It took five years of legal wrangling before everyone was satisfied.'

Which meant at some point he'd be expected to marry again. Someone *suitable*. But until then he was free to date Hollywood actresses and glamorous models. And she'd be able to read all about it.

Marianne shivered again.

Why did they settle for that? Surely the knowledge they'd slept with a prince didn't make it hurt any less to know they were only a body to him? It had hurt her.

'Still feeling cold?'

'A little.'

'Perhaps we should rejoin the others.'

Marianne nodded. She stood up and the chair grated against the paving. The comparative warmth of the sitting room hit her immediately she entered.

'How's your headache?' the professor asked.

'Much better.' Marianne smiled, though it didn't feel quite natural. Her emotions seemed balanced on a knife edge. 'The fresh air was a good idea.' She carefully unwound her wool wrap and folded it neatly on the chair.

'Excellent.'

His attention quickly returned to Dr Leibnitz. It seemed quite incredible to Marianne that it wasn't immediately obvious to the two other men she'd changed somehow.

She sat herself on the edge of the sofa and glanced over at the clock on the mantelpiece. It was late—and she wanted nothing more than to go back to the Cowper Hotel. Her feet were aching and she'd lied when she'd said her headache was better. It was sitting behind her left eyeball just waiting to explode.

How much longer was the professor going to be? Her mind seemed to be buzzing, incapable of following their conversation. Then, quite suddenly, it was over.

'I'll give you a few days to discuss everything with your wife,' Seb said, standing up, 'and then I'll ask you for your decision.'

The professor nodded. 'Yes, indeed.'

'Perhaps you could talk directly with Johann von Renzel, my chief of court. Assuming your decision is in the positive, he'll be able to organise accommodation and your travel arrangements.'

In her heart of hearts Marianne knew there was no decision to make. And, incredibly, the thought of going to Andovaria was no longer such an ordeal. Seb hadn't set out to hurt her. She believed that—so she couldn't hate him any more.

If she ever really had. There was a part of her that would always love him. A part that was angry. And a part of her that felt sorry for him. He might live in a gilded cage, but it was a cage nevertheless. His whole life defined by an accident of birth and he hadn't had the courage to break out.

'You're very quiet,' the professor observed as he settled himself in the back of the taxi.

Marianne turned her head to look at him. 'You've already made your decision, haven't you? You've decided to accept.'

He closed his eyes, looking more tired than he'd ever admit. 'If we pick our team carefully…'

Marianne looked out of the window at the Randall before the taxi slipped out into the London traffic.

Seb shrugged off his jacket and dropped it on the nearest chair, untying his bow-tie at the same time. He walked over to the window and stood, one arm resting on the frame, looking out across the terrace.

That had been, perhaps, the hardest conversation of his entire life.

Good, though. It was as though a loose end had been finally tied.

'Will that be all, sir?'

Seb turned. 'Yes, thank you, Warner.' The butler had started to move away when Seb noticed Marianne's pink wrap lying on the chair just inside the door. 'No, wait.' He strode over and picked it up, amazed that the light rose perfume she'd worn that evening still clung to the fibres. He hadn't even been aware he'd noticed her perfume.

'Could you see that this is packaged up and delivered to Dr Chambers at the Cowper Hotel?'

'Yes, sir.'

'I believe they'll be checking out by ten o'clock tomorrow.'

'Yes, sir. I'll see that it's delivered tonight.'

The door shut behind him and Seb turned back and idly fingered the selection of books the Randall had provided. Crime, thrillers, non-fiction, classics… Nothing on the shelf grabbed his attention.

In fact, he felt…restless. Hell only knew why. The evening had gone well. He was almost certain that Professor Blackwell would accept… which was, in the main, what he'd stopped over in London for. Viktoria would be delighted. But, still…he felt dissatisfied.

It was probably remembering. Practically a

full decade of royal responsibility since he'd last seen Marianne. The last time he'd acted solely in line with his own inclination.

Seb lay down on the sofa and rested his head back on the armrest. Five weeks. That was all they'd had. Five weeks before his life had been turned upside down and he'd been thrust relentlessly into the limelight.

Tabloid fodder. That's what she'd called him. For the first time he paused to wonder what she'd thought when she'd first discovered he was the crown prince of Andovaria.

It wasn't comfortable thinking.

He rubbed a hand over his tired eyes. And he *was* 'tabloid fodder'. Every last thing he did was reported somewhere. He only had to speak to some woman for rumours of their affair to be circulating round the better part of Europe by the morning. It probably took a week for the same information to reach the States.

Seb sat up abruptly and swung his legs down to the floor. He reached out for the phone and keyed in a nine to obtain an outside line.

'Nick?' he said as soon as a sleepy voice answered. 'Have I woken you?'

'No, but I'd just about given up on you. Are you still coming over?'

He leant forward and rested his elbows on his knees. 'I'll be with you by lunchtime tomorrow. Just don't put me in the room with the leaking roof again,' he said, waiting for the crack of laughter which wasn't long in coming.

'How long are you staying this time?'

'Just the weekend. I've got to be in Vienna by Monday lunchtime for a meeting with a trade delegation and then I'm off to the States straight after that.'

'How long for?'

'Six weeks, all but a couple of days.' Seb sat back again and briefly contemplated telling Nick he'd seen Marianne. He brushed a tired hand across his face. Somehow it felt too difficult— and he wasn't ready to be questioned about her. He didn't know how he felt.

But he was fairly certain he knew how Marianne was feeling.

She'd heard him out—and, perhaps, that had been more than he'd deserved. But she still felt he'd let her down and, *damn it*, he had.

CHAPTER FIVE

Seb leant forward and tapped the driver of his car on the shoulder. 'Stefan, stop here, please. I need to stretch my legs.'

Obediently his driver brought the car to a halt, the one immediately behind doing the same, and Seb turned to Alois, sitting beside him. 'Can you take my briefcase up to my private apartment? Leave these with Liesl and I'll work on them again later.'

'Sir.'

He shuffled the papers he'd been working on back into his briefcase and handed them across with a nod of thanks. Then, leaving his jacket on the seat, he opened the door and stepped out into fresh air.

It was good to be home. Really good. Seb drew the air into his lungs. Travel might broaden the mind, but home was good for the soul. *Who'd written that?* He couldn't remember, but it was so true.

He really loved this place. It seemed to envelop him every time he stood inside its protected boundaries. Poltenbrunn Castle, with the Alps rising majestically behind it, was rather a spectacular building in a truly breathtaking setting. Most of the time he took it for granted, but sometimes, like now, after a longish absence, he was struck how incredibly fortunate he was to live the life he did in the place that he lived it.

Seb stood back and allowed the cars to snake their way up to the castle, before following on foot. Of course, six weeks of hotel suites, paparazzi with their telephoto lenses focused on every window and the constant companionship of the men assigned to protect him probably had a lot to do with his relief at being home. At least here he was afforded a modicum of privacy.

His smart leather shoes prevented him from doing anything other than sticking to the main path, but he took the longer route around the great lake. It was an incredibly beautiful vista. And one he'd loved since he was a child.

He'd spoken to people over the past couple of

weeks who seemed to have no sense of place or purpose, people whose lives had been shattered through no fault of their own. And all this was his. 'In trust for future generations' —but his.

Just as he was occasionally reminded of the beauty of his home, so was he reminded of the responsibilities of his position. Few people were able to influence so much or bring about such change simply by virtue of who their ancestors were. At nineteen he'd balked at that, wished for a different life…

Seb looked across the lake towards the oldest part of the castle. *He'd wished for Marianne*. At nineteen he'd accepted he would be the next sovereign prince of Andovaria, but it had cost him. And seeing Marianne in London had reminded him how *much* it had cost him.

The sturdy grey stone of the old keep looked so permanent and dour as compared with the later more aesthetically pleasing additions. In less than a week she'd be there.

Seb paused at the brass sculpture of Maestoso Bonadea XII, his father's favourite stallion, and moved his hand down the smooth muzzle. It was going to be strange to know

Marianne was at the castle…every day. Close, but not close.

Perhaps it was because their relationship hadn't been allowed to run its course that he felt…

Heck only knew what he felt.

Seb screwed his eyes up against the mid-afternoon sun. Since he'd seen her in London he'd thought about her pretty much constantly. How much worse would that be when she was actually here? Just knowing that she was a five-minute walk away from his private rooms…

He turned abruptly away and rounded the bend, his feet slowing as he saw a solitary female figure coming out of the woodland area. There was something about the way she was walking that made him stop completely and his stomach want to jump in both directions simultaneously.

It was *her*. Incredibly.

And he knew the moment Marianne had moved close enough to recognise him. Her body seemed to tense and then she resolutely carried on up the path.

Seb pulled a hand through his hair and searched his mind for something suitably casual to say. He'd spent the last six weeks thinking about her, wondering whether she'd changed her opinion of him, wondering whether she still felt anything for him…

Just wondering. Idly. And now here she was. And he wasn't prepared for how it would feel to see her against the backdrop of his home.

Marianne stopped a few feet away from him, her shoulder-length blonde hair drawn back into a casual pony-tail. She looked so absurdly young. Incredibly beautiful.

And he wanted to kiss her. He knew exactly what it felt like to slide his hands over her body and feel her lips warm and moving against his. In fact, he knew more than that. He knew what it was like to be inside her. To wake and watch her breathing. All of a sudden his skin felt several sizes too small for his body.

He drew a hand round the back of his neck to ease out the sudden tension. Nervous as any adolescent. Unsure what he should say. What he shouldn't.

The edge of Marianne's long white cotton skirt caught in the summer breeze and her pony-tail flicked out behind her. Then she smiled.

'Y-you weren't supposed to be here until

next week,' he managed in a voice that sounded hoarse.

She shook her head. 'I'm here to set up the computers before the professor arrives next week. I…came on ahead.'

'Oh,' He nodded. And now he felt foolish. *Even more foolish.* His mind was refusing to work and he didn't seem to be able to stop looking at her. She wore no make-up and he could see the pale translucency of her skin, the purple smudges beneath her dark eyes. And he remembered how those eyes had looked dilated and drowsy with passion. 'How long have you been here?'

'Ten days.'

He brushed his palms down the back of his trousers. 'I've been away—'

'I know.'

She smiled again and twisted a strand of hair behind her ears. 'Did you have a good trip?'

'Yes. Yes, I did. Thank you.'

Marianne nodded, more as though she wanted to encourage him than anything else. 'I'm glad.'

Then she moved as though she intended to continue past him and Seb felt compelled to stop her. 'D-do you have everything you need?'

'Yes.'

'Good. That's good…' His voice disappeared into a husky whisper. Seb pulled the air into his lungs. This conversation was becoming faintly ridiculous.

'I'm being really well looked after. Princess Viktoria is very organised. She thinks of things I might need before I've thought of them.'

'That's good,' he said again, and inwardly groaned. Somewhere across the Atlantic he must have lost the ability to talk to a beautiful woman.

Or perhaps it was just the ability to talk to this one?

He'd have done better if he'd known she was already at the castle. He could have prepared himself. Steeled himself for how it would feel to see her again.

'She's very enthusiastic about the project.'

'Yes, she is.' He pulled a hand through his hair and cast her a shaky smile. 'Sorry, I'm not making much sense, I know. I'm jet-lagged. I need to get some sleep. Perhaps then I'll be able to string more than a couple of words together.'

Marianne's dark eyes lit with a glimmer of sudden laughter and he knew that whatever had been between them ten years ago was still there. For him at least. The only confusing thing was how he'd ever managed to walk away from her.

Perhaps, at nineteen, he'd not been aware how rare it was to feel such an intense connection to another person? But he knew now. In ten years he'd not come close to experiencing anything like it.

'How long was your flight?'

Even her voice was sending warm shivers through his body. Reminding him of everything his sense of duty had robbed him of. 'Eight and a half hours. Just under eleven hours door to door. And there's a six-hour time difference.'

Again her smile tugged at him and he wanted to touch her. Once he'd been allowed to do that. He could have cradled her face in his hands and kissed her.

'No wonder you're tired.'

'I'm shattered, but it's better if I can keep myself awake until evening.'

Seb knew the right thing to do was to smile and move away. Move and keep moving. But…there was something about her blonde beauty and the intelligence that shone out of her dark sexy eyes that acted like a siren's call. So difficult to resist. Almost impossible.

Smile and walk away.

As a working royal, Seb was an expert at that. He knew exactly how to finish conversations without causing offence or embarrassment. But…he seemed powerless to do what his head was telling him.

And he knew the reason why hadn't changed. *He liked being with her.* Still. She made him feel alive. Happy. As though he could do anything, achieve anything. *Be* anything he wanted.

Blood pumped through his veins and he felt acutely aware of everything around him. The trees seemed larger, the grass greener. The air felt cleaner, sharper.

The last time he'd felt like this he'd walked up to her on the steps of Amiens Cathedral. Made her talk to him, invited her to go to a coffee shop.

Seb pulled an agitated hand through his hair. 'I'd better get back or they'll be sending out a search party.'

Marianne nodded.

Walk away. The voice of caution was getting

weaker and in its place was the whisper of temptation. *Where was the harm in talking to her?*

'Are you out for a walk?'

She held up the flask of coffee she'd been cradling against her. 'Having a break. Remembering it's still summer. It's cold in there,' she said, gesturing back towards the castle.

'Sorry.'

Another smile. She had the most incredible mouth. Soft and sensuous. And when she smiled it seemed to short-circuit his brain. 'It's not your fault they didn't put a good heating system in.'

Seb could feel his lips stretch into an answering smile. There was nothing he could do to stop it. 'It's not a desperately good heating system in the newer part either.'

'Isn't it?' Marianne's eyes skitted away towards the castle. It was the first indication that she might not be as comfortable as she appeared. That small movement gave him a little confidence.

'But it's nowhere near as dreadful as the heating in Nick's place. I think he should put thermal underwear as the dress code on all invitations.'

Her eyes came back, warm brown…and questioning. He still wanted to kiss her. Did she know that? Could she tell from the way his eyes hovered on her mouth despite his best intentions?

'I stayed with him for the weekend after I'd met you. He sends his regards.'

'Oh.' Her hands clasped and unclasped the flask.

Seb saw the movement and noticed the way her eyes yet again moved past him. Marianne wasn't comfortable—any more than he was. But she wasn't walking away from him either…

'Are you heading for a specific spot?'

Her eyes swung back. 'Spot? Oh…for coffee? No. I wouldn't know where to go. This is the first time I've come in this direction. I've normally walked through the parterre and up to the pavilion.'

'Do you mind if I join you?'

The slight widening of her eyes suggested that her decision might swing either way, but after a moment she shook her head. 'No. I don't mind. There's enough coffee for two. That is, if you like it white with sugar.'

He didn't. He liked it strong and black. And he didn't even want a coffee. This was crazy. What was he doing? Exactly what he'd promised himself he wouldn't do.

'We might as well sit here,' she said, slipping

the rucksack off her shoulder. 'It's an amazing view from here.'

Seb reached out for her rucksack. 'Come with me.' He turned and led the way across the grass, completely ignoring the damage he was doing to his shoes.

Marianne followed him—or followed whatever she'd put in her rucksack, he didn't really care. The sleep that had been pulling at his eyelids all the way from the airport seemed to have disappeared and he felt…reckless. Younger.

And he wanted to show her his home as it was meant to be seen. 'Here,' he said, stopping and putting her bag down on the grass. 'What do you think of this one?'

He watched as she turned to look down at Poltenbrunn Castle. From here its twelfth-century keep was entirely obscured and you were left with a fairy-tale castle.

'This looks very familiar.'

'It's the image that's most often used on post-cards. All seasons. All times of day. But I've never seen a photograph yet that quite captures the essence of the place.'

'It looks like Rapunzel might appear any

minute at one of those turret windows,' she said, unwrapping her jumper from around her waist and setting it out on the ground.

'Maybe that's what I ought to do with Isabelle. Lock her in the tower,' he said in answer to the slight raise of her left eyebrow.

'Your sister?'

'Younger sister,' he agreed, sitting down beside her. 'She seems to ricochet from one disaster to the next. Locking her up might be the perfect solution. I'll put it to her.'

'It didn't work for the witch who tried it.'

Seb laughed. 'I'm sure it wouldn't for us either. She'd be bound to do something outrageous. Though it can't be much worse than disappearing for a week.'

'You disappeared for longer than that.'

True.

Seb turned and watched her as she unscrewed the top of her flask and separated the two cups. He hadn't compared himself to Isabelle before. Maybe she was that unhappy? 'Isabelle is older than I was,' he said slowly. 'She's twenty-two.'

'Not so very old.'

No, not old, but by twenty-two he'd accepted his destiny. He'd been enthroned as the sovereign prince and he'd married Amelie.

'Do you want some?' Marianne asked, holding up the flask.

He'd married Amelie when he'd been in love with Marianne. Twenty years old, with a very heavy heart, he'd done his duty. Seb swallowed. 'If there's enough. It might help keep me awake.'

She said nothing, but poured coffee in both the cups. 'What time did you leave New York?'

'About eleven. I left immediately after the charity dinner finished.'

Marianne looked up. 'Whatever time was that? Are you sure everyone else wouldn't rather have had a good night's sleep before setting off?'

'I imagine they're pleased to get back as early as possible. Most of them have families to come home to.'

Her brown eyes widened. 'But you didn't ask them?'

'It's their job—'

'To protect you and to do what you want,' she interrupted smoothly, passing him the larger of

the two mugs. 'Yes, you've told me that before.'
Her mouth quirked. 'You must be insufferable to
be around, Your Serene Highness.'

Seb took a sip of the coffee he didn't really
want and studied her. There was a new confidence about Marianne now. A quiet conviction
that she had something worth saying. He liked it.

'You don't have a particularly good opinion of
royalty, do you, Dr Chambers?'

Her smile broadened. 'Let's just say I had a bad
introduction to the species.'

'Thanks.'

Marianne laughed. 'You're welcome.'

Seb sipped his coffee. He liked this. People
rarely laughed around him, he realised, and they
certainly didn't relax or treat him the way they
would any other human being.

Except Nick.

But Nick was a friend from school. And Nick
was someone who understood how his life
worked. He was one of just a handful of people
he could trust and the only person he'd ever
confided in.

Which made Marianne particularly unusual.
She didn't seem to see him as a ruling prince and

she certainly treated him like any other human being. And she was equally trustworthy, but with far less reason.

Marianne's smile faded and she turned to grab her rucksack. He had the strongest sensation she was hiding from him and he longed to be able to reach and turn her face back so he could see her eyes. If he could see her eyes he'd know what she was thinking.

'I'm afraid I've only got one of these and it's lunch,' she said, pulling out an apple.

'Now?' He glanced down at his watch. 'You're having lunch now? I thought you said Vik had been looking after you.'

'She has,' Marianne tossed the apple in her hand, 'but not so well she forces me to come for lunch. I forgot the time. I only noticed it when I started to feel chilly.'

'That engrossed?'

She nodded, the sparkle returning to her eyes. 'You've no idea what you've got down there. It's incredible. Yesterday I found a list of Konrad I of Thuringia's possessions in 1236.'

'And he was?'

Marianne tucked a strand of hair behind her

ear. 'Oh, sorry. He was a *Hochmeister* of the Teutonic Order.'

Seb found himself smiling again as the enthusiasm rang in her voice. It was infectious. 'You really do love what you do.'

'Of course. What's the point of doing something if you don't love it?'

Duty. The single word slid into his mind.

'You're a long time dead. Eliana says that. She believes life should be as fun as you can make it,' she said, taking a bite of her apple.

When she said it like that he agreed, but it was a philosophy that ran completely counter to his training. He sat silent for a moment. Life—*his* life—wasn't about fun or enjoyment. It was about fulfilling one's duty, never losing sight of his responsibility to his country and his family.

Marianne let the silence stretch out. Unbelievably, sitting with Seb, talking to him, felt…all right. When she'd first seen him as she came out of the wood she'd panicked, but it was fine.

In fact, it was better than fine. She was here on her own merit, she was doing a good job and she was talking to Seb as though he was an old friend. Almost comfortable.

'So why this view?' Marianne asked, staring down at the mellow bricks. She preferred the more austere, permanent feel of the old keep. 'I mean, it's lovely, but why do you love this particular one?'

Seb glanced across at her. 'My father used to bring me here.'

'Just you and your dad?'

He nodded. 'From about the age of eight. During the school holidays he made a point of it. Once, maybe twice a week.'

Marianne took another bite of apple, happy to watch him. It was easy to see why she'd fallen so hard and so quickly. Seb, prince or not, was gorgeous.

He took a sip of his coffee. 'Other than that I never got to see him alone. There was always someone somewhere wanting a piece of him.'

'And now it's your turn.'

He looked his question.

'Someone somewhere wanting a piece of you,' she clarified with a swift smile, before taking another bite of her apple.

She couldn't even begin to imagine what his life must be like. How would it feel to be surrounded by other people—at all times—and yet be essentially alone? Set apart from birth?

Did that feel lonely?

It was easier to imagine Seb as an eight-year-old striding out with his dad. Marianne plucked at the grass beside her. 'Did your sisters mind you having their dad to yourself?'

Seb wiped a tired hand across his face and she smiled. He looked exhausted.

'Isabelle, no. She was that much younger. Viktoria might have, I think. But I was his heir. It was all part of the training regime.'

And that about said it all. Marianne looked over the top of her apple. 'Even though you're not the eldest,' she said, watching for his reaction.

It was quick to come—and she loved that about him. Loved not having to explain what she meant. 'You don't approve of male succession either? Why doesn't that surprise me? How about,' he said with a sudden glint in his eyes, 'if I tell you it's been part of our tradition since 1138?'

'So was having a married sovereign and you changed that.'

She watched him fight his laughter. 'But that was only a tradition since 1654.'

'Of course, that makes all the difference,' Marianne said, tipping out the dregs of her coffee on the grass beside her. She looked up and smiled.

She'd missed this. Missed *him*.

What would have happened if she'd met him for the first time today? Would he have wanted to spend time with her?

Probably.

When he looked at her…

Marianne wrapped her fine cotton skirt around her bare legs. And would she have wanted to spend time with him? She glanced over as his fingers tipped his empty cup upside down on the grass.

What would Seb say if he knew that he was still the only man she'd ever made love to? That his lean hands had been the only ones ever to move across her body?

Marianne turned away and bit down on her lip. It was finished. It didn't matter how attracted she was to him—or him to her—there could never be any long-term future. She wasn't 'suitable'. He'd told her that.

'Can I ask you a question?' she said suddenly.

'Of course.'

'Wh-when you said your parents knew about me…'

'Yes?'

'Does that mean people know now?' Marianne turned her face to look at him. 'I mean…do people know that I'm the person you were with in France and—?'

'Why do you ask?'

She shrugged, trying to appear nonchalant. 'I wondered if Princess Viktoria might have…' Marianne shook her head and let her fingers stroke the grass beside her. She wasn't sure what Seb's sister had been thinking. It was just a suspicion.

'She might remember your name,' he said, handing his cup across. 'My mother certainly will. And the protection services will both remember and know absolutely that you're the same woman.'

'And be watching me?'

'They watch everyone that stands close to me. It's their—'

'Job,' Marianne finished for him. She twisted the lid back onto her flask. 'I don't like it.'

'Marianne, as soon as your life touched mine it was inevitable. You'll have been under low-level surveillance ever since we met in France.'

'Isn't that an infringement of my personal liberty or something?' she asked as she stood up. 'I thought it was illegal to keep information on people without their knowledge.'

'My safety is paramount.'

Her eyes narrowed and she swung round to look at him. 'Because you're *so* important. I keep forgetting that, don't I, Your Serene Highness?' She bent and picked up her jumper, shaking the grass and the mud off it. 'You're important and I'm not important.'

'It isn't my fault,' he said quietly. 'I was born to this.'

No, it wasn't his fault. But she didn't have to like it. It really bothered her to think that unseen people had been watching her movements—over a ten-year period. Perhaps making files on her she'd no knowledge of. Free to say anything they liked about her, make judgements, without any threat of redress.

And did 'they' know she'd been pregnant? Had 'they' decided not to tell him? Marianne rolled her jumper into a tight tube and fed it into the rucksack along with her empty flask.

It would be better if she kept angry. Kept remembering why she couldn't let herself fall under his spell for a second time.

'They only use the information if they think you're a threat.'

She swung her bag on her back. 'Can't you just tell them I'm not the bomb-planting type?'

Seb smiled and her stomach flipped over. 'They don't listen to me. I'm merely the object to be guarded.'

He was gorgeous. And what he was saying was true, she supposed. Every friend he made, all the people he met—everyone vetted for their suitability.

What a *horrible* life.

She'd thought that so many times since she'd met him again in London. It looked different in the photographs. Then you saw the beautiful surroundings, the clothes, the exotic locations you were never likely to see in person, and she'd felt…well, angry. But there was another side to it.

Even knowing that your life was at sufficient risk to warrant the level of protection Seb had must be unpleasant, let alone living with the day-to-day consequences of it. Personally she'd much rather have her life with its smaller worries about mortgage payments and lifting bamboo flooring.

'We'd better start heading back before they send out a search party. If they find me with you I'll never be able to convince them I'm not a threat to national security.'

'It's not personal.'

What a daft thing to say. It *was* personal. Of course it was personal. How could it be anything *but* personal? She'd had the temerity to fall in love with the Andovarian crown prince and been a marked woman ever since. And it was *extremely* personal not to be considered good enough.

Well, news flash, it wasn't a vacancy she wanted to fill. Maybe her guardian angel had known what she was doing when she made it impossible for her to refuse coming to Andovaria.

All she had to do was to keep focused on what had brought her here. It *was* a great career opportunity. And the professor *did* need her. And maybe, just maybe, she'd return to England and be able to get on with her life without feeling that the best part of it had already happened.

'Where are you staying?' he asked as they walked back across the grass.

Marianne looked sideways at him. She'd hoped he already knew that. 'In one of the guest suites. I thought you'd okayed it.'

'I've been in New York.'

'I know, but…' She bit her lip. That was what had worried her when Princess Viktoria had insisted. That and something indefinable in the way his sister had looked at her. 'Princess Viktoria said it would save me a great deal of time each day, not having to get through Security.'

'I'm sure it does.'

'Was that wrong of her?'

'Why would it be wrong?'

She didn't know. That was the whole point. They were on his home territory, not hers. But there'd been something about Princess Viktoria's expression that had made her wonder whether she suspected her reason for being in Andovaria was not entirely due to the discovery of twelfth-century artifacts.

Of course, she could be being over-sensitive. She was incredibly nervous about being here. Nervous about seeing Seb again. Nervous about…pretty much everything and that was bound to throw everything out of kilter.

Marianne tucked a loose strand of hair behind her ear. 'I'd booked a room in a hotel, but Princess Viktoria—'

'I'm glad she did.'

'You are?'

'Of course. There's no point running the gauntlet of the paparazzi every day when you don't need to.'

'No.' And that did make sense. She'd been shocked to see how many people seemed to be waiting at the private entrance to the castle. 'Is it always like that?'

Seb shook his head. 'They're waiting for Isabelle. She'll be home for my mother's fiftieth birthday celebration—and they all know it.'

'And are they there day and night?'

'Only if they can't get in,' Seb said drily, 'and they do more than wait. They jump out of bushes, they try and bribe the staff here, get friends of friends to talk. Anything to make sure they get a picture no one else gets because that's the way they earn their living.'

'Does she know that that's what's in store for her?'

Seb stopped at the bronze statue of the horse and looked across at the sweeping drive which led up from to the private entrance. 'She's a fool if she doesn't. The official Press pack are hard enough to accommodate, but the paparazzi are something else altogether.'

'I'd hate that.'

Seb looked across at her. 'We all do. They're so single-minded it can be quite frighten-ing…I'm sorry—'

'It's fine.'

'But not your problem and I shouldn't have—'

'I don't mind. It's interesting.' And she liked him talking to her. Telling her things about his life and the way he felt about it.

It was funny, but until this moment she hadn't registered how little she'd actually known about Seb while they were together in France. She'd poured out all the details of her life. Talked about her parents, her village, her school, her dreams for the future. But Seb…had said nothing. Couldn't, she now realised.

Which meant he must have been constantly editing what he was saying. Thinking of things to say and then realising he couldn't. She'd been so incredibly stupid.

'What are you thinking?'

Marianne bit back an almost hysterical laugh. There was no way she was going to tell him that. He didn't need to know she'd found a new humiliation. 'Nothing.'

'Please. I'd like to know.' His voice was deep and quiet. 'I can always tell when you're unhappy.'

Marianne looked up and the expression in his eyes made her heart beat erratically. She felt cold, frightened and incredibly small. There was something going on between them she didn't understand and couldn't seem to control. *How could she be falling for him now?*

'Marianne.' He breathed her name and it was as though it was expressing an emotion he didn't have any other way of communicating.

Slowly, giving her plenty of time to move away, Seb stretched out his hand and his knuckles brushed lightly against the side of her face. 'You're so beautiful.'

Beautiful. That single word throbbed through her body. She wanted to hear that. Needed to hear it.

His thumb moved gently against the side of her jaw, barely touching, and yet every nerve in her body had screamed to attention.

'So beautiful.' Barely a whisper. It almost seemed to hang in the air.

His eyes held hers. Dark, dark brown. His pupils wide and black. Easy to fall back in love with him. Easy to forget how alone she'd felt when he'd left her alone in Paris.

Left her.

Seb had left her. Beautiful meant nothing. It meant he wouldn't mind going to bed with her. It didn't mean he loved her. Or that he wanted to know her dreams or share them with her.

'No.' Marianne pulled away.

Seb shot a hand through his dark hair. His eyes looked bleak and, for one moment, she thought he was going to say something.

She shook her head. 'I can't,' she whispered.

Seb nodded and then he walked away.

Marianne raised one shaking hand to her lips and stood there. She felt weak…and foolish… and exposed.

He'd wanted to kiss her.

She knew it. And the truth of it was…she'd wanted to be kissed.

In the distance she saw his tall figure disappear between the archways and she knew that if she could have called him back she would have.

Marianne tightly shut her eyes against the tear that had spilled over onto her cheek. She was in one almighty mess. She wasn't over loving Seb—and she probably never would be.

So, what was she going to do now? She felt as though a fierce wind had blown through her body and had left her buffeted.

CHAPTER SIX

S EB stretched out the aching muscles in his back. He'd worked himself hard in the gym, but he knew that it was tension that was causing the problem—and that Marianne was the reason for the tension.

What had he been *thinking*? He stood under the hot jets of water and let the rivulets run down his naked body. He needed the shower to wash away more than the dirt and grime from ten hours of travelling.

The trouble was he hadn't been thinking. He'd been feeling. His hand balled into a fist, but there was nowhere to vent his frustration. *Damn it!*

'Seb?'

He leant forward and turned off the shower as Viktoria's voice penetrated the sound of the water.

'In the shower. I'll be out in a second,' he called back, reaching for a towel off the warm rail. He slung it low round his hips and then picked up another from a pile on the nearby table.

He emerged drying his hair with vigorous movements as his sister looked up from the magazine she was reading.

'I see you're featuring in this one,' she said drily, holding out the open page.

Seb spared the article a brief look and continued drying his hair. 'Liesl brought them for me to see. There's a fair bit about Isabelle in the ones below.'

'Who's the brunette?'

'The wife of someone I met in Los Angeles.' He finished drying his hair and tossed the towel across the back of a nearby chair. 'Don't worry, her husband was standing to the left of her. I'm not dragging the family into disrepute.'

'Just out of shot.' Viktoria closed the magazine disdainfully and set it down on the table. 'I hate that they can get away with that. It's completely misleading.'

'You and I both know that kind of nonsense sells magazines,' he said, walking through to his dressing room and pulling out a pair of denim jeans and a folded black T-shirt, 'and let's be grateful it's me in that one and not Isabelle.'

He heard his sister's snort of derision and smiled. Viktoria had never put a foot out of line in her life. She'd made an approved, dynastically sensible marriage and appeared reasonably content in it. If she and her two boys made increasingly lengthy stays at Poltenbrunn Castle, who was he to comment?

Seb pulled his T-shirt over his head and walked back through to see that his elegant elder sister was looking unusually pensive. And he was fairly certain he knew why—and, for the first time in a long time, it wasn't about Isabelle's exploits.

He paused in the doorway. 'Is this a conversation we ought to have over tea and cakes or is it more of a whisky and soda one?'

'I need to talk to you.'

'About?' He moved to sit down opposite her and tried to keep his body language as relaxed as possible.

'Dr Chambers.'

His sixth sense hadn't failed him. He'd known this conversation was inevitable from the moment Marianne had said his sister had placed her in one of the guest suites.

'What about her?'

'Who is she?'

'Professor Peter Blackwell's right-hand woman.'

Viktoria rubbed at her exquisitely plucked eyebrow. 'I don't doubt that, but—'

'And the grown-up version of the girl I met in France.'

At that her expressive eyes swung round to look at him. There was no surprise in them, just an incredulous disbelief. 'Why did you bring her here now?'

'I didn't; you did. You were the person who insisted on Professor Blackwell.'

Viktoria's elegant fingers nervously twisted one of her pearl earrings. 'And you didn't know your ex-lover was a close colleague?'

'No.'

Her mouth pursed. 'Somehow I find that hard to believe—'

'I don't honestly care what you believe,' Seb said, his patience exhausted. 'Vik, I'm tired. I've been travelling for something like ten hours and I don't need this. I had a relationship with Marianne Chambers ten years ago and we haven't been in contact since. What do you think is going to happen now?'

'You do know we can't afford another scandal. The annulment of your marriage rocked the monarchy…'

'I know.'

'…and with Isabelle cavorting around Europe with her skiing instructor—'

He cut her off more forcibly. 'Yes, I know.'

Viktoria made a monumental effort to smile and stood up. 'I know you'll do the right thing. You always have before.'

Yes, he always had before.

'I'll leave you to rest before dinner. You must be exhausted.' She reached for the door handle. 'But, Sebastian, please don't come down dressed like that. You'll make everyone else feel uncomfortable.' Then she hesitated. 'Incidentally, I put Dr Chambers in one of the guest suites because of the paparazzi outside…in case you were thinking—'

'She told me. She's not a fool, Vik, she had a very good idea why you'd done it.'

'How did she tell you?'

Seb pulled himself to a more upright position. 'I met Marianne outside. In the grounds. Maybe an hour ago.'

'And?'

'We spoke. I've come in for a shower. There is no "and".'

Viktoria looked at him closely. Two deep frown lines marred her otherwise smooth forehead.

He smiled and yet it was completely mirthless. 'I'm perfectly aware that you think I've brought my latest lover to the castle to rather tastelessly coincide with our mother's fiftieth birthday, but do you honestly think Dr Chambers would settle for the kind of relationship I could offer her?'

'Many do. You haven't lived like a monk since Amelie left.'

'Viktoria,' Seb took a deeply calming breath, 'Dr Chambers is here at your invitation. Whether you put her in the guest wing, a house in the grounds or a hotel in Poltenbrunn, Marianne wouldn't be interested.'

'You're sure?'

'Look at it from her point of view, Vik. She was an innocent eighteen when I met her, not some publicity-seeking starlet. What do you think she thinks of the way I treated her?'

His sister's mouth twisted in unwilling comprehension. She nodded. 'I'm glad. Not that you treated her badly, of course, but that you haven't deliberately brought her here. There are enough column inches devoted to our declining moral standards without adding anything else to the mix. And please don't forget what I said about changing for dinner,' she said before shutting the door quietly behind her.

Seb pulled himself out of the chair and walked through to his bedroom.

Damn!

He'd seriously underestimated Viktoria's ability to retain all facts pertaining to anything that threatened the stability of the Andovarian monarchy. And Marianne had certainly done that.

Seb stretched himself out on top of his bed and bent his arm over his eyes to shade them from the sun streaming through the windows. At nineteen he'd tried hard to persuade his father and uncle that he'd fallen in love and that the way he felt about Marianne was more important than anything else.

Their arguments had been strong and unequivocal. Their views on the secondary importance of love in a royal marriage fixed. Eight hundred years of tradition and history balanced against a girl he'd only just met. And he'd been young and overawed by what was immediately ahead of him.

In the end he'd allowed himself to be swayed by their experience. And, perhaps, they were right. Amelie had been desperately unhappy. She'd found royal life unbearably confining—and she'd been groomed to fill such a position.

He rubbed his fingers round his aching eye sockets. He knew what his duty required. He was acutely aware of it. At some point in the not too distant future he would need to marry again—and he couldn't afford to make a second mistake. Public sympathy would only stretch so far.

His consort would have to be someone who was comfortable with being Her Serene Highness the Princess of Andovaria. Someone who could embrace this kind of rarefied life and find it satisfying.

And that wasn't a woman who was more comfortable in jeans and wore her hair in a casual pony-tail. Nor was it a woman who believed that enjoyment should come before duty.

It wasn't Marianne.

But, knowing all that, he had nearly kissed her. Today. Out by the statue of his father's horse. Not that the venue was important. What mattered was the overwhelming sense of compulsion.

Seb sat up abruptly and pulled a hand roughly through his hair. When he was around her he couldn't seem to stop something flaring between them. And even at nineteen he'd known that if he couldn't offer the possibility of forever, he had nothing to offer her.

Marianne woke particularly early—and she knew why that was. She lay for a moment, listening to the sound of birds outside, and then restlessly pushed back the covers. Hours of thought and she was nowhere nearer deciding what was the best thing to do.

Everything that had persuaded her to come to Andovaria was still valid. There were exciting historical discoveries to be made. Peter and Eliana were packing up their home in Cambridge and were arriving in five days. The professor was relying on her to be his support. Relying on her. And she owed him that support.

Nothing had changed.

Except…

He'd so nearly kissed her. Marianne padded

over to the enormous wardrobe and pulled out her white towelling dressing gown. She wrapped it round her body and pulled the belt tight.

And she'd *wanted* him to kiss her. She didn't begin to understand how that was possible. Not when she'd spent the last ten years clawing back her self-esteem. Marianne walked through to the small kitchen area and picked up the kettle.

It was weak to want Seb to kiss her. And she didn't do weak. Not any more. She filled the kettle by aiming the water carefully into the wide spout rather than removing the lid, focusing her entire concentration on not missing a drop.

Ten years of protecting herself from being hurt again. Ten years of striving for other people's good opinion as though that would somehow make Seb's rejection of her less painful.

And in one single moment—the moment when she'd realised that if Seb kissed her she'd kiss him back—all that work had been swept away on one gigantic wave of emotion. She felt as though the foundations of her entire adult life had been shaken—and she was left desperately vulnerable.

Marianne pushed the tap lever to 'off' and carefully settled the kettle back into its cradle. She felt so sick inside, deep inside. Too hurt to cry. Too confused to think. Since meeting Seb everything had been shifting about so much she almost didn't know how she felt about anything.

But the sad truth was that no one had ever matched up to him. For ten years Seb had been the 'gold' standard by which she'd judged other men. And when they'd wanted to kiss her she'd felt entirely neutral about it.

Sometimes she'd let them and other times she hadn't. But it had never felt compelling. Or particularly sexy. Or…anything. For ten years she'd been emotionally switched off. Shut down to life.

Marianne reached across and lifted down a white china teapot and the small canister containing English tea. She'd no idea whether the tea was something Princess Viktoria had arranged especially for her because she thought she was sleeping with her brother, or whether the Blue Suite always had English guests, or whether everyone in Andovaria always drank English tea, but she was glad to find something familiar.

Because nothing else was. Seb lived in a completely different world to her. Her entire house in Cambridge would fit inside this guest suite twice over.

But what she really wanted was everything back the way they'd been in France. She wanted that magical feeling of closeness. Marianne hugged her arms around her body. It didn't matter how much she told herself that their time together had been an illusion—she still wanted that feeling of connection.

She was twenty-eight years old. *Twenty-eight*. And she'd never come close to feeling anything like it since—and deep down she was scared she never would. Perhaps she never would find someone who'd make her feel the way Seb had.

Marianne rested her hands on the edge of the sink, letting the stainless steel bite into her hands. It would probably help if she could let herself cry, but everything she felt had been buried too deep and too long for tears.

In one decisive movement she went back to her wardrobe and pulled out her navy blue suitcase. Empty now except for the red box she kept hidden in the inside zip pocket. Marianne placed the case on her bed and unzipped the side, before throwing it open.

She knew what was there. In that narrow side-pocket. It came with her everywhere she went. Always. But it felt more difficult to look at it now. Her fingers shook slightly as she pulled out the red box and pushed in the tiny catch that held it shut.

The white gold heart Seb had given her nestled against the black velvet. It was a beautiful thing but, more than that, what it represented had been beautiful. Marianne lifted it out and let the links of the chain run through her fingers.

Seb *had* loved her when he'd given her this. She honestly believed that. She might have been naïve and foolish…and young, but she was sure he had loved her. Maybe not with the depth of passion she felt for him, but there'd been something…

She had to cling to that. Because otherwise everything was a lie. The first time he'd held her hand pretending to search for her life line. The time he'd cradled her face in his hands and kissed her. When they'd nervously hired that first room and shut the door…

Marianne felt the first hot tear burn her cheek. She didn't attempt to wipe it away, but sat there letting it, and the ones that followed, scald her skin like acid.

She loved him.

She still loved him. And she loved the baby they'd made together. If Jessica had lived she would have given her entire life to make everything perfect for her.

Marianne's shaking fingers felt for the fragile catch and carefully opened the locket. Inside was a tiny photograph of a perfect little girl. Eyes shut. Looking more like a china doll than a real baby.

Her baby. Hers and Seb's.

The pain sliced through her like a chef's knife. The speed and the freshness of it always came as a surprise to her.

And she knew, looking down at the tiny picture, that the pain would never go away. Not even if she lived into very old age. Always she'd carry the grief of losing her child…

Doubly painful because she'd not even had the chance to know her. She'd held Jessica just the once. Tiny, perfect and still warm.

Just the once…

The sound of a car startled her and Marianne flicked the locket shut. She closed her hand over it protectively and went to look out of the window. It was barely six in the morning and yet there were any number of people standing in the forecourt. All in formal suits and standing beside sleek black cars with smoky windows.

Marianne turned away and went to put the locket carefully in its case. She was no clearer now about what she should do than before, but crying had helped a little. She had so much to mourn. The loss of a daughter…and of a dream.

She left the suitcase open on the bed and walked over to re-boil the kettle. If Eliana had seen her do it she'd have objected on the grounds that it concentrated the minerals in the water, but Marianne didn't care. Her hands went through the practised procedure of making tea and then she stood, with her hands cradled around its warmth, and watched the commotion outside.

Commotion was the wrong word. There was no sense of pandemonium, just a calm sense of procedure. There were three cars parked in an orderly row, the distance between each of them exact. And they were flanked by riders on motorbikes in a precise formation.

Marianne hid behind the window dressing and watched with a quiet fascination. In the time she'd been at Poltenbrunn Castle she'd not seen anything quite like this. There was a noticeable shift in the posture of the men. They stood a little straighter, looked a little more alert. Marianne took a sip of tea, her attention captured by what was happening outside her window.

Her breath caught in her throat as Seb stepped into the picture frame of her window. He was dressed in a sharp black suit and he was flanked by Alois von Dietrich on his right and two grey-suited men either side of them both.

Marianne shrank back further into the folds of the curtain. He looked exactly like the photographs she'd seen in so many publications. The complete personification of what a modern royal should look like.

He stopped and said something to Alois before ducking down inside one of the cars. Marianne continued to watch as the door was shut and Alois walked round to sit next to him.

Only then did everyone move. It was as though they were working through practised procedures—which they probably were. Then the montage moved off as though it were one. Safe from detection, Marianne stepped out from behind the curtain and watched more openly as the cars and outriders snaked their way towards the private exit.

Marianne gripped her mug convulsively. She hadn't needed anything else to confirm how completely different his life was from hers, but this was a visual illustration of the gulf that separated them.

She'd hoped that coming to Andovaria would finally give her 'closure' and it seemed that someone somewhere had been listening.

CHAPTER SEVEN

THE professor pushed his glasses higher on his nose and frowned. 'Can't make this out at all. Marianne, what do you think?'

She picked up the neatly typed sheets the professor had given up on and quickly skimmed the contents. 'It's suggesting there was a second castle in Andovaria owned by Ulrich von Liechtenstein.'

'Does it pinpoint where?'

Marianne shook her head and reached for the pencil she had tucked in her pony-tail, putting a tiny note in the margin. 'Doesn't say. But, since he died in 1278, it's the right time frame.'

'Interesting.' The professor pulled off his glasses and rubbed at his eyes. 'I've had enough for today. I think I'm going to go and have supper with Eliana. How about you?'

Marianne shook her head. 'I'll finish looking

over these, then I'll have a shower and head for my bed. I'm tired.'

He nodded and Marianne reached for a jumper and pulled it over her head. She liked it in the open-plan office when everyone else had gone home. She felt safer there, more cut off from what Seb was doing than when she was in the guest wing. And she found it was better if she actively tried not to know where he was.

Today there'd been the sound of a helicopter taking off and returning and that had been bad enough. Her imagination had immediately started to picture where he'd been going.

Even the little information she'd unavoidably picked up about his life had begun to alter her perception of him. He worked hard. Long, long hours. Leaving early and returning late most days.

Marianne spotted another mistake in the translation the professor had been given so she made a small note in the margin and returned the pencil to her pony-tail for safekeeping. She kept working systematically through it, sheet after sheet, even when the last of the team had long gone.

It was all so fascinating. Names she vaguely recognised from other sources were becoming three-dimensional human beings with every paragraph. She rubbed a tired hand over her eyes and pushed herself to continue. One thing she'd learnt over the past two weeks was that it was better not to go back to the guest wing until she was ready to fall into bed. Sleep only came when she was completely exhausted.

Seb didn't feel tired. A visit to support an inter-racial community project in the north of Andovaria, followed by the royal opening of the largest neonatal unit in central Europe hadn't done anything to use up his restless energy.

He stood at the window and looked down at the guest suite. Everything was in darkness—which meant Marianne was sleeping. He glanced down at his watch. Five minutes after two in the morning. What the hell was he doing? He'd got the annual diplomatic reception in something like eighteen hours. He ought to try and get some sleep himself.

But…he knew there was little point. He simply wasn't tired.

And he'd thought about Marianne all day. He'd had a spectacular view of the keep as he'd flown out today and it had started his mind wondering, yet again, what she was doing. Whether she was still excited by what they were discovering.

And he'd wondered how long she intended to stay. Just knowing she was there was difficult. Particularly when he'd determined not to ask Viktoria anything about the project. This was her 'baby' and she would leap to a million and one conclusions if he expressed too much interest in it.

Seb opened the door of his private apartment and wandered out along the corridor, nodding at the security guard who was patrolling along it. He'd no particular destination in mind, just a desire to be doing something. The four walls of his private sitting room had begun to feel as though they were closing in on him.

He walked down the curving marble stairs and along the west gallery, past the state dining room and on into the north drawing room. Lights were low and the castle was quiet except for the ticking of clocks and the creak of old floorboards.

During the day this was a bustling hive of activity, but at night it was eerily quiet. And, perhaps, more beautiful. On the nineteenth-century walnut table was a novel by Nicholas Sparks. Seb picked it up and turned it over in his hand. Something Viktoria must have been reading and had left out.

He idly read the back cover and laid it carefully down, exactly as she'd left it. Seb glanced again at his watch. Twenty past two. It seemed as if the whole castle was sleeping except him….

Which meant it couldn't do any harm if he went to look at what was happening in the keep storerooms. He quickly walked through the inter-connecting rooms that led to the panel that provided the only access to the keep's lower storage area.

Light glimmered under the almost closed doorway. He pushed it open, expecting to find someone had left the office light on—but found Marianne. Seb hesitated, his hand on the door handle.

A wise man would walk away.

She was asleep, her head resting on her arms and her drink cold beside her. He smiled and let go of the handle. 'Marianne,' he said softly, not wanting to startle her.

The only response was a sort of snuffling

sound that made his smile stretch further. He moved her coffee out of harm's way and touched her lightly on the arm. 'Marianne. Wake up. It's the middle of the night.'

She emerged rather as he'd always imagined the dormouse did in *Alice in Wonderland* but her first word wasn't 'treacle'. Marianne frowned and stared at him wide-eyed. 'Why are you here?'

'Curiosity.' He smiled because he couldn't help it. She looked so delightfully rumpled. Most of her naturally wavy hair was still pinned in its ponytail, but there was enough that had escaped to make the look anything but tidy and she was wearing a green pencil like a stick in a cocktail drink.

'What time is it?' she asked, rubbing at her neck. 'I must have fallen asleep.'

She most certainly had fallen asleep. There were red squares across her cheek where the texture of her wool jumper had left its mark. Seb glanced down at his watch. 'Twenty-five minutes past two.'

Marianne frowned. 'Why are you here?' she asked again.

'I told you. Curiosity.'

'In the middle of the night?'

Seb fought the desire to laugh. He loved

being with her. Just talking, being close to her, and he felt the pressures of his day lift away. 'It is my castle,' he protested. And then, 'I can't sleep.'

'You ought to work harder,' she said, still rubbing at her neck. 'I must have been here hours. Is it really twenty-five minutes past two?'

Seb held out his watch so she could see.

'Jeepers.'

'What's that mean?'

Marianne looked up questioningly.

'Jeepers? It's not a word I know.'

'It means… Oh, I don't know. It means it's twenty-five past two and I ought to be in bed.'

Seb smiled as she tried to ease out her body. 'Stiff?'

'Like you wouldn't believe.' She reached out for her coffee. 'This is stone cold.'

'Not incredibly surprising, is it? You probably made it hours ago.' Seb took the mug from her fingers and walked over to tip the contents away in the nearby sink. 'Why are you still here? Is Professor Blackwell a hard taskmaster?'

Marianne shook her head. 'I stayed on a bit later to finish reading this.'

'Is it that interesting?'

It was on the tip of her tongue to say that she was only reading it because the professor hadn't been able to, but she stopped herself in time. 'Possibly.'

'Noncommittal,' Seb said with a glance over his shoulder, his hand reaching for the kettle. 'Do you want another coffee?'

'You're going to make me coffee?'

His smile twisted. 'I do know how.'

'Yes, I know you do,' she began, stopping abruptly when she noticed the deep glint of amusement in his eyes. 'I suppose you'd better, since you probably don't get much practice.'

Seb laughed and it was as though someone had popped a bottle of champagne inside her stomach. She rubbed at her arms in an effort to distract herself.

'Cold?'

'Yes, I am.' Though why, she didn't know. She was wrapped up warmly in a thick hand-kitted sweater, whereas Seb was in a fine wool jumper and dark black moleskin trousers. He looked good in black. Almost Italian with his dark hair and dark eyes.

'Probably because you've not been moving around.'

'I suppose.'

'Do you still have your coffee with just the one sugar?' he asked, with a quick glance over his shoulder.

Marianne nodded. *Still*. He'd made coffee for her before.

He came over to the table and handed her a mug, before sitting down with his own. 'Tell me what you've found.'

'In this?'

He nodded.

'This is just a translation of one of the documents we found last week.' Marianne took a sip of her steaming coffee.

'And?' he prompted.

'And…' Marianne put her mug down on the table and pulled one of the sheets towards her. 'It's possible that Ulrich von Liechtenstein built a castle in Andovaria.'

Seb smiled across the top of his mug. 'Should I know his name?'

'Possibly not,' Marianne conceded, fighting the smile that was tugging at her mouth. 'Unless you've been nurturing a secret passion for knights in the thirteenth century. It's not conclusive, though, but a possibility.'

'Is he a well-known knight?'

'Not particularly,' Marianne said, tapping the papers on her desk. 'I had a pencil here somewhere—'

'It's in your hair.'

'Sorry?'

Seb leant forward and pulled the green pencil out of her pony-tail. 'In your hair.'

'Oh,' Marianne said, accepting the pencil and tapping at her head. 'I do that sometimes.'

'Yes, I know.'

And that was the trouble, he did know. Just being near him made her feel tingly and slightly edgy. He knew so much about her.

She pulled her eyes away and fiddled with the papers on the desk. 'Ulrich was born in 1200 and knighted by Duke Leopold VI of Austria in 1223. There's very little known about his life, but we do know he owned a castle in Liechtenstein—'

'Makes sense. Him being a von Liechtenstein.'

Seb's voice was teasing and Marianne ignored him as she added, 'As well as two others. One of which might have been somewhere in Andovaria.' She wrote another note in the margin.

'Stop now.' He laid his hand over hers. 'It's late.'

His hand was warm and his touch sent shivers coursing through her spine. 'You're right. I ought to go to bed.' As soon as the word 'bed' left her mouth images poured through her heightened imagination. Marianne picked up her coffee. 'I want to make an early start in the morning.'

'Why?' Seb's dark eyes were watching her, making her feel uncomfortable. Making her feel as if she were comprised of nothing but hormones.

And there was no 'why'. She'd only said it because she'd wanted to cover up the 'bed' thing. Marianne took another quick sip of coffee. 'What are you doing tomorrow?'

Seb smiled. 'Today,' he corrected.

'Today, then.'

'At ten fifteen I have a meeting with my mother—'

'With your mother?' she echoed, not quite sure he'd heard him correctly.

Seb nodded. 'The summer ball is in honour of her birthday, so I think she should have some say in what happens.'

'Yes, but…' She looked up to see his eyes laughing wickedly. Marianne gripped her mug a little tighter. 'Do you often have "meetings" with your mother?'

He grinned across at her. 'Not usually. When she's at Poltenbrunn we meet over dinner.'

Of course they did. Marianne wasn't sure how she felt about being teased by Seb. She was trying so hard to keep herself aloof, to remember all the reasons why she had to keep some distance between them. But it felt good…

Seb took a final sip of coffee and put his empty mug down on the table. 'And in the evening it's the diplomatic reception.'

'Oh.' Marianne finished her own coffee and quickly stood up. She'd absolutely no idea what a diplomatic reception was, other than it sounded as if it might be one of those state dinners she'd seen on fly-on-the-wall documentaries made about the British royal family. 'Shall I wash your mug?'

Seb hand it across to her. 'Thank you.'

'Is it fun?' she asked. 'The diplomatic reception.'

'Not often.' Seb stood up and moved closer. Marianne could feel his eyes watching her even though she had her back turned towards him. 'It's very formal. There's a guest list of around nine hundred people and I get to speak to them all.' He smiled. 'At least it feels that way.'

Marianne looked over her shoulder. 'So not fun?'

'More like an endless wedding reception. The first three hours are the worst,' he replied wickedly. 'But it's only annual, thank God.' He paused. 'Let's get out of here.'

'Pardon?'

'Leave here,' he repeated. 'You're right, it's cold. We must do something about getting some heaters in here.'

'Th-this part is fine. It's only cold now because the heating is off.' She knew she was rambling, but her stomach had started fluttering. 'Go where? It's the middle of the night.'

His smile had her blood pulsing. 'I could give you the guided tour.'

'Of the castle?'

'Well, not all of it. It's an unusually large building.'

Her eyes fell to her shoes as she wrestled with her conscience as to whether she should go with him or not. Obviously 'not' was the most sensible decision. But…to see the castle. And to see it with Seb.

Seb held out his hand. 'Coming?'

And it seemed the most natural thing in the world to put her hand inside his. 'I want to see the ballroom. Wasn't it the largest room in Europe when it was first constructed?'

He threaded his fingers through hers. 'You've been reading the guide book.'

Perhaps it was because it was the middle of the night, but Marianne felt as if she was in a bubble. It was as though this time was borrowed time. Outside of normal rules and considerations.

He led her out into the north drawing room. 'You're familiar with this room?' he said, looking down at her.

Marianne nodded.

'Well, I hope you've appreciated the stuccoed ceilings.'

She looked up. 'I'm afraid I didn't notice the ceilings.'

Seb smiled and pulled her on and out into the impressive hallway with the large curving marble staircase. Paintings of hunting and battle scenes lined the walls in big, heavy frames. Marianne hated them all. She paused at a particularly gruesome one.

'Why do you have these here?' she asked.

'Because my great-great-grandfather hung them and no one has dared move them since.'

Marianne laughed. 'Which one was he?'

'Prince Hans Adam II. He reigned from 1853 to 1917. There's a portrait of him in the long gallery, looking particularly worthy.'

'Do you know the names of all your ancestors?'

Seb released her hand and opened the doors to a room on the left, flicking on the light switches. 'All of them. It was part of my royal training. I had a tutor who made up a tune to help them stick in my head.'

A tune. This whole night was beginning to feel rather surreal.

'So eventually someone will have to learn all about you.'

He smiled, his eyes glinting. 'Scary thought, isn't it? Now, this is the grand drawing room. And I particularly dislike the red silk-covered walls in here.'

Marianne stared past the rococo furniture and

on to the huge double doors at the end of the room. 'What's through there?'

'The blue drawing room. One day I intend to paint it all green for the hell of it.'

Her breath caught on a gurgle of laughter.

'In my father's time court etiquette still demanded both parts of those doors were opened every time he wanted to go from one room to the other.'

His voice was laced with humour and Marianne turned to look at him. *Seb really loved this place*. He knew its history and secrets and he loved it. Connected to it through generations.

Not the playboy prince of the tabloid press, then. Marianne could almost hear another crack appear in the shield she'd built around herself. There wasn't a great deal of it left to protect her.

'You've been very careless with Andovarian traditions.'

'Not me. That one went when my father married my mother.'

Marianne looked up questioningly and caught the laughter in his dark eyes. 'Both sections only had to be opened when the sovereign prince walked through. Lesser mortals could manage with just the one door and, since my mother was considered a lesser mortal…'

'She didn't like it,' Marianne finished for him with a smile. 'Neither would I.'

Seb turned to look at her and it was one of those moments where the air seemed to disappear from the room and it became, quite suddenly, difficult to breathe.

And he felt it too. 'Marianne,' he murmured, his eyes appearing almost black.

Her laughter died. *He was going to kiss her.* And she wanted him to.

'P-please,' she said on the tiny amount of air she had left in her lungs. She didn't need to say what for—which was just as well because she wasn't sure what she was asking for.

Marianne saw him swallow before he stepped back. It was the safest option, probably the right decision. Marianne opened her mouth, and then shut it again. She couldn't think of a single thing to say as regret flooded her.

'And through here is the long gallery,' he said with a swift movement towards a door to the right.

She didn't want to kiss him, didn't want to unleash all the feelings she still had for him—but she didn't want this either. It felt wrong.

Her feet moved slowly towards the long gallery. It was pretty much as she has expected. Windows to one side and portraits to the other.

Seb had switched on the lights and turned back to look for her. 'This is the way to the ballroom.'

Why was she doing this? There was no possibility of friendship with Seb. She wanted more. She wanted him to love her. To hold her, keep her safe and *love her*.

As though he knew she was deciding whether to continue with their middle-of-the-night exploration, he stayed where he was, turning to look at one of the portraits. 'This is Prince Josef Johann who by all accounts was a thoroughly unpleasant character.'

Marianne walked closer and looked up into a beautifully painted oil portrait. She couldn't resist it. She felt as if a million skeins of the finest silk were pulling her towards it. Towards Seb. Inevitable.

'He reigned from 1772 to 1781. Not particularly long, but long enough to seduce half the female population and ensure that the Rodier genes were well-established in Andovaria.'

'He's handsome,' Marianne smiled. *But not as handsome as Seb.* Not as sexy.

'And this is his son, Prince Hans Adam I.'

'The man who put the pictures along the staircase?'

Seb's dark eyes glinted down at her. 'You're not paying attention. That was Prince Hans Adam II and the paintings are far too modern. This Hans Adam ruled from 1871 to 1805 and he was a great traveller and amateur botanist.'

'And less handsome.'

'Quite. He seduced far fewer Andovarian maidens and, in fact, I think his preference lay in quite another direction.'

'Is seducing maidens part of the job description, then?' The question left her mouth before she'd realised what she was saying. Marianne bit her lip.

His voice was deep, sexy. 'No. Not since 1914.'

Marianne looked up, startled, and saw his eyes alight with laughter. She felt her skin heat.

He lifted his hand to stroke her cheek. 'You still do that?'

'What?'

'Blush.'

'Not often.'

Seb laughed. 'Only when we're discussing the seduction of maidens?'

'Something like that,' she returned, wrapping her arms protectively round her waist.

'Still cold?'

Marianne let her arms fall back down to her sides. 'No. Not really.' And then, because he was watching her closely, 'A little. Is it peculiar to know you're related to all these people?'

'Not really. You have as many ancestors lurking behind you. I just know who mine are, that's all.'

Marianne walked on further down the long gallery. It was rather amazing to think that all these people's lives were interlinked. One life leading on to the next until they reached Seb. The latest in a long line of rulers.

She glanced up at him, searching for the distinctive Rodier family features. Dark hair, dark eyes and strong cheekbones. 'Do you have a portrait?'

'Oh, yes. Inescapable duty. I was added to the rogues' gallery when I succeeded my father.' Seb walked on a few steps. 'This is my grandfather. This is my father…and this is me.'

Marianne's shoes sounded loud on the oak floorboards of the long gallery. She gave all the portraits a cursory inspection, before stopping next to Seb. She looked briefly at him and then at the painting of him.

She wasn't sure what she'd been expecting, but this painting wasn't it. Every other portrait, it seemed, had shown grown men, confident, steely and ready to take on the challenge of their rule.

But Seb's portrait showed a boy. Tall, unmistakably a Rodier with his dark hair and dark eyes…but a boy, who was uncomfortable in his stiff uniform.

She let her eyes wander back along the corridor. So many paintings. A monarchy that stretched back hundreds of years. Then she looked at the young Seb. He'd taken his place, but he looked as if he was playing a man's role before he was ready.

Was that how it had felt? She knew he'd been young and he'd told her he hadn't felt in control of what was happening to him—and finally, seeing this, she believed him. Really believed him.

Marianne swallowed the hard lump in her throat. 'What's the blue sash and jewelled cross?'

'That's the Grand Star of the Order of Merit of the Principality of Andovaria.'

She nodded, but she scarcely heard him.

'It's very heavy. I don't think I've worn it since.'

'You look so young.'

She'd wanted to know why Seb had left her—and this was the 'why'. It was a calling—almost as sacred as one to the priesthood.

'I was young. That was painted just before Christmas the year I met you.'

Marianne swallowed again. 'Will you change it? Later, I mean?'

'No.' Seb shook his head. 'That's a moment in time. My first official portrait as the ruling prince. There are any number of other portraits.'

'Are there?'

'I sit for at least one a year.'

A different life. A very different life. Marianne pushed up the sleeves of her jumper. She wanted to run away and hide somewhere. She'd known for ten years his life was different. She'd known it when she'd first arrived at Poltenbrunn Castle. And when she'd seen him leave the castle in one of those sleek, purring cars.

But now she *felt* he was different.

'And through here,' he said, crossing to another pair of double doors, 'is the ballroom. Currently set up in readiness for the diplomatic reception.'

Light and airy because of the phenomenally high ceilings, Marianne's eyes looked upwards at the intricate mouldings. Then they travelled to the huge mirrors…

No!

She gazed at her reflection, horror-struck. She looked as if she'd been dragged through a hedge backwards. Her hair was falling out of her ponytail and her light summer skirt looked stupid with her heavy knitted jumper.

Marianne quickly pulled the elastic band out of her hair and ran her fingers through her natural curls. And then, of course, wished she hadn't as she caught a glimpse of Seb's laughing eyes in the mirror.

'I look like the wicked witch of the west,' she said by way of an excuse.

'You look beautiful.'

Seb had said that before…in exactly the same way. And his brown eyes did that thing they did that made her feel as if she was burning up from the inside out.

And she wanted to cry. Marianne swung her head away so that her hair would give her some privacy. 'Is this where the summer ball takes place?'

'All these tables will be cleared away after tomorrow and an army of florists will set about transforming it.'

Marianne felt as if it were someone else speaking. She wanted to go back to the relative sanctuary of the guest wing. She wanted time alone to think about what she'd seen. Understand what she *felt*. 'When is Princess Isabelle arriving?'

'She spoke to Viktoria. They've agreed it would be better if she arrived at the last possible moment. There'll be so many other people arriving then…'

Marianne nodded and then she tensed as she felt Seb's hands on her arms. He spun her to face him. 'What's the matter?'

'It's nothing.' She drew in a short breath and let it out slowly. It *was* nothing. Nothing new. 'It's an amazing room,' she said on a croaky whisper. 'Thank you for showing it to me.'

His right hand slipped up to her shoulder and the other hand gently pushed back her fine blonde hair. With one thumb he brushed across her eyelids as though he could erase whatever it was that was making her look so sad.

His warm hand moved from her shoulder to tilt her chin. 'What have I done to make you sad?'

Marianne let out her breath on a broken laugh. 'Nothing. It's not you. It's me.' She tried to step away from his intense scrutiny, but he didn't release her. 'It's not your fault. It's mine. M-my fault.'

'What's your fault?'

He looked completely bemused and she couldn't really blame him. Seb didn't possess the single most significant fact about their time together. He didn't know they'd made a baby together. So for him it was all relatively simple.

Her eyes searched out his dark ones. 'I didn't understand. You told me in London, but I didn't really understand.' She tried hard to find the words that would convey what she was trying to say—without telling him about Jessica. He didn't need to know that. 'I've finally seen you as a prince. I really believe it. I don't think I did before. Not really.'

He brushed his knuckles over her cheekbones and ever so gently down her cheeks.

'This is all so impossibly big.' Marianne took another breath in on a hiccup. 'Your life is different from mine. You belong here and I d-don't.'

'Marianne.'

Her name on his lips unlocked the first tear. It carved a warm furrow down her cheek and Marianne tried to turn her head away from his incredible eyes. His thumb moved gently across it and his warm hands held her steady.

'I—I understand now what you meant in London. I needed to see this to really understand. For ten years I've been so angry at you for something you couldn't help.' She took her shaking bottom lip between small white teeth.

She wanted to die. Not really. Of course, she didn't really want to die, but she wanted him to stop looking at her that way. That mixture of compassion and tenderness. It hurt to see him look like that. It reminded her…

Another tear spilled onto her cold cheek and she felt his right hand burrow deep in her hair, moulding itself round her scalp. She should pull away, but it was what she needed. Seb was the only person who had any hope of understanding how bereft she felt. How utterly…*hopeless*.

Because, finally, she had to accept she could never have played a part in Seb's future. Whether he loved her or not—she was not part of this…however you chose to describe this.

She came from a long line of farm labourers. Their marriage certificates signed with their 'mark' rather than a signature. Only when free education had been introduced had anyone from either side of her family done anything other than live a hand-to-mouth existence in extreme poverty….

Not better. Not worse. Just *different*.

Seb kissed the teardrop away, and then her right temple, each kiss seeming to brand her as his. Warm and moist. She wanted him. Had always wanted him. But she wanted the man, not the prince.

She heard the small moan that came from deep within her throat, felt the lean muscle tone of his back as her fingers splayed out across it.

And then he kissed her lips. Soft and question-ing at first. He drew back and looked deep into her eyes. He was waiting, asking for her permis-sion. Marianne closed her eyes and leant into him.

His strong hands moved to cradle her face and his thumb moved against her softly parted mouth before he kissed her. Hard. Possessive. She opened her mouth to him the merest fraction and allowed her tongue to touch his.

She remembered this. *Exactly* this. The feel of his body pressed up against hers, the taste of him, the scent of his skin…

It was as familiar as walking from one room into another—and yet so, so sexy. Easy to forget that Seb Rodier didn't really exist. That the man she was kissing was Prince Sebastian—a man who'd left her because she wasn't 'suitable'.

She pulled back, her body suddenly tense.

'Marianne?' His dark eyes were so close to hers. She could feel his breath. 'What is it?'

'I—I can't do this.'

His thumb moved across her sensitised lips and she forced them not to open beneath it. 'What can't you do?'

'This. Us,' she whispered. 'It wouldn't work. I wouldn't be happy.'

Seb stepped back and pulled his hands through his hair. 'We need to talk—'

'We don't, Seb.' Marianne cut him off. 'There's nothing to talk about. What we had in France was special, so it's natural we should still feel something for each other, but you can never go back.' She tried to smile. 'It wouldn't be the same.'

CHAPTER EIGHT

A DOOR banged in the next room and Marianne looked round. 'What's that?'

'One of the night-time security staff, I imagine.'

Marianne drew in a shaky breath. 'He'll be wondering what we're doing here. We'd better go.'

'I imagine he knows.' Seb rubbed his hand across the back of his neck, reluctant to tell her how public their kiss had been. 'There are security cameras in all the state rooms.'

'Wh—'

'Most of the castle, in fact.'

Marianne wrapped her arms around her waist. 'We're being watched? Now?'

'As long as we're in the state rooms. Come.' He held out his hand, but she didn't move towards it. 'There are no security cameras in my private rooms.'

'What about the guest wing?'

'Not inside the suites themselves. Come with me,' he repeated. She didn't move. Her eyes were wide with shock—and he could understand that. He was used to living with people watching his every move and tended to forget it was happening. But for Marianne it was a new experience and, no doubt, unnerving. 'This way,' he said quietly.

She followed him wordlessly until they reached the grand staircase. 'I know my way from here. I can—'

'We can talk in your suite or in my rooms—I really don't care which you choose, but let's finish this. One way or another.'

Her eyes flickered with some emotion he didn't recognise and then he saw the resignation.

'This way.'

Her eyes darted around, presumably looking for security officers who might be patrolling this area of the castle, but she needn't have worried. The very fact that their kiss would most certainly have been watched on the security monitors meant they'd see no one now. The staff at Poltenbrunn were adept at not being seen.

He kept a tight hold on her until they reached the door to his private apartment. Marianne looked over her shoulder at him as he held the door open, then she walked in. Her shoulders were tense and her beautiful face as strained as he'd ever seen it.

Seb pulled his hand through his hair, unsure quite what he hoped to achieve. It was clear, though, that they couldn't continue as they were. Every time they were together something flared between them. Lust? Love? He didn't know. But he'd tried hiding from her and that hadn't worked.

He switched on a side-lamp and the warm light pooled around it. Then he moved across to dim the central lights. 'Whisky?'

'Please. A small one.'

Seb glanced over his shoulder. Marianne stood in the centre of the room, one arm clutching at the elbow of the other. *Why did she look so broken?*

'Ice?'

'Please.'

He put the ice in the bottom of the glass and then poured in the whisky. 'It's a single malt,' he said, handing it across to her.

'Thank you.'

'Make yourself comfortable,' he said, turning away to pour a second drink. There had to be an easy place to start this conversation, but he was damned if he could think of it.

What he really wanted to know was what she wanted from their relationship and, since he didn't know what he wanted from it himself, that was a difficult question to ask. They *had* options. Options that hadn't been there a decade ago.

Seb turned round to find Marianne hadn't moved. One hand was fiercely clutching the glass tumbler, the other clutching at the hand that held it. *Surely this was about more than having been caught kissing on camera?*

He walked over to her. 'Marianne…' He stopped and looked down at her hands, knuckles white with the pressure she was putting on the glass. 'We used to be able to talk to one another—'

'I talked. You didn't, Seb.' The expression in her usually soft brown eyes shocked him. It wasn't anger. It was hurt. Deep, profound hurt.

'Sit down,' he said, moving across to an attractive grouping of sofa and chairs. 'Please.'

She moved stiffly, her hands still tightly closed around her tumbler. He waited until she'd chosen her seat and then he deliberately sat opposite, where he could see her face.

Marianne took a small sip of her whisky and he could see she made a conscious decision to relax. Her hands loosened their grip and her shoulders visibly lowered. He sat, silently, waiting until she was ready to continue.

'I only realised just now how difficult it must have been for you when we were together in France. Not to be able to talk about any of the things that mattered to you.'

Seb went to speak and then realised he'd nothing to say.

'When I told you about the house I grew up in…' she stopped and took another sip of her whisky. '…you said nothing about where you'd grown up. Because you couldn't. I'd not noticed that before. I'm so stupid.'

Seb eased out the muscles in his neck.

Marianne's hair swung down in front of her face and her fingers moved against her glass. 'I feel such a fool for not noticing.'

He cleared his throat and thought of how to explain what had happened back then. He'd already tried to explain in London…

Or thought he had. Perhaps he hadn't? All he'd really done was present a calm justification of what he'd done to her ten years ago and why. He hadn't explained anything other than his reasons for leaving her.

Maybe that was where this conversation needed to begin?

'It didn't feel awkward,' he said slowly. His smile twisted as he tried to search out the words. This—being honest—was difficult. He'd deliberately not thought much about their time together. Once it was over there hadn't seemed much point. 'I liked hearing you talk.'

Marianne looked up, her hair falling back to softly frame her face. *She looked like an angel.* And he still liked hearing her talk. Liked the way she didn't simply agree with everything he said.

'I'd never met anyone who'd gone to the local non-selective school. Or who'd lived in a house that shared a wall with anyone else's.'

Her eyes flicked across to him. She was listening. And listening hard.

His fingers traced the rim of his tumbler. 'It fascinated me that if you did your piano practice before eight o'clock in the morning Mr Bayden from next door would bang on the wall.' He smiled, hoping she understood what he was trying to say. 'I didn't want to talk about me. I wasn't conscious of not being able to, just of not wanting to. Does that make any sense?'

There was a small delay before she nodded.

Seb let go of the breath he'd been holding, then continued more confidently. 'And I knew that as soon as I told you who I was…everything would change. I didn't want things to change. I liked being Seb Rodier. I liked being able to walk to the local café and find a bench by the Seine and watch the street performers…'

He heard her small sniff and saw her brush her sleeve against her nose. He'd not seen a woman do that since…she'd done it when she'd been helping him pack his bag.

Damn!

Seb put his whisky down on a side-table and ran both hands through his hair. He'd made a mess of everything. When he'd left her he'd honestly meant to contact her. More than that— his real plan had been to return to Paris. She'd known that. Forty-eight hours, he'd told her…

Only what he'd found at home had been life-changing. Very different from anything he'd expected.

'What happened to you?' he asked quietly.

Marianne's hands moved against the glass. Her shoulders moved in a defensive shrug. 'When you didn't come back?'

'Yes.'

She brushed the back of her hand across her nose again. Seb stood up and walked across to his dressing room, coming back with a starched white handkerchief.

'And?' he said, holding it out to her.

Marianne looked at it and then gave a tiny smile. 'You know, the rest of the world use paper tissues.' But she took it and held it balled against her glass.

He waited. She *would* tell him what had happened to her…if he waited. He was confident of that.

'When you didn't come back…'

'Yes.'

Her eyes flicked up to his and then away. Seb still waited, his body braced to hear whatever it was she was finding so hard to say.

She took another small sip of whisky. 'When I couldn't afford to stay at our hotel any longer I met Beth and we pooled our francs to settle the bill.'

He'd forgotten the bill. Seb pulled a hand

through his hair. *Dear God, forgive him.* He'd left her to pay for their hotel room.

'Then we travelled to Honfleur together. Monsieur and Madame Merchand were lovely.' She drew a shaky breath. 'And Honfleur is a really beautiful place. Old. Lots of tall, thin houses.'

He nodded, though he'd no idea what Honfleur was like.

'And the little girl I was helping look after was sweet. I'd have been all right, I think, only my period didn't come.' She looked across at him, watching for his reaction. 'I was regular as clockwork, so it was strange, but I thought it might be because I was missing you. Sad, you know? Sometimes that messes up your cycle.' Her fingers moved against the glass. 'Anyway, that's what I thought.'

Pregnant!

Marianne had been pregnant? Seb's mind was one expletive. Of all the things he'd expected Marianne to say, this hadn't figured anywhere. 'You were pregnant?'

Marianne nodded. 'Beth and I went to buy a pregnancy test on the Monday after we got there.

We were really embarrassed to ask for it.' She wiped her nose against the handkerchief. 'It was positive. Very clear. A dark blue line.' She moved her hand in a single stroke downwards.

There was probably something he should say here, but Seb couldn't think of anything. *Marianne had been pregnant.* Eighteen, pregnant and in a strange country.

'I told the Merchands I had to go home. I didn't tell them why. Just that I needed to go home.'

He nodded.

'They were very nice about it. Helped me sort out a ticket and Beth came with me to the station.'

He watched as she crumbled. First her hands twitched against the glass and then her bottom lip trembled. He saw her catch at it with her small white teeth. Then the tears started to fall in earnest.

And he sat there, powerless to do anything. He wanted to walk over and hold her, but he didn't quite dare.

'She died, Seb.' Her voice was so soft and laced with a kind of despair. 'Jessica died.'

Marianne's words hit him hard. He wasn't quite sure what to react to first. He'd left

Marianne *pregnant* with no easy way of contacting him. And their baby had *died*.

She took another shaky sip of whisky, and the glass tapped against her teeth. 'Sorry. I wasn't going to tell you—'

'*You're* sorry? What have you got to be sorry about?' He moved then, coming to sit beside her on the sofa. He took the glass from her agitated fingers and placed it on the side-table, before reaching out to hold her hand. She didn't pull away. In fact, her fingers twitched inside his. 'Our baby died?'

'Jessica. I called her Jessica.' Marianne nodded and another tear welled up and slowly, so slowly, spilled onto her cheek.

Seb lifted a hand to smooth back her hair, his fingers lightly brushing across her left temple, and then he drew her back until she rested against him. He felt solid. Strong. 'Tell me.'

Marianne couldn't. Not for a minute or two. The words wouldn't come. She could hear the solid, steady beat of his heart. One hand gently stroked her hair and his fingers brushed against her neck. The other held her hand.

She felt so tired. So very tired.

'Everyone wanted to know why I'd come back early.' Her words sounded slurred and her eyelids felt heavy.

'What did your parents do?' His voice was a distant rumble.

'Cried. My mother cried a lot. She was so disappointed…and embarrassed.' Seb's fingers moved against the base of her neck.

Marianne felt a light kiss on the top of her head. So soft she might have been mistaken. She fumbled for the handkerchief and tried to sit more upright. Seb let her go and she blew her nose.

'Do you want some more whisky?' Seb asked, nodding at her empty glass.

Marianne reached out to pick it up off the table. 'Please.'

She watched him walk over to the drinks table and put in first the ice cubes and then a generous dash of the amber liquid. *What was he thinking now?* Was he angry with her? He didn't seem angry. Though why she thought he would be she didn't know. Only that so many people had been.

Marianne brushed her hair off her face and waited for him to walk back with her drink. *Two whiskies*. Her mother would be disappointed by that, too. 'Thank you.'

He smiled and sat back down beside her. His eyes were warm. 'Is that when you went to live with professor Blackwell and his family?'

Marianne nodded. 'My mother couldn't cope. She thought everyone in the village was talking.' She gave a swift, humourless smile. 'They were, too: "Pregnant without a boyfriend in sight". She thought I'd be better off in a hostel for girls in a similar position.'

She swirled the liquid round in her glass, watching it crash against the ice rocks. Funny how you could do that with words. Say one thing and mean something entirely different. Her mother had *said* that she'd be better off in a hostel, but what she'd *meant* was that it would be better for her.

And she'd been so frightened by that. She'd gone from being a 'golden' girl to being something that needed to be hidden away. She'd spoilt everything. All talk of university had been over.

'But my aunt Tia rang Eliana and I went to live with her... and her family.'

Seb pulled her in close against him. She liked that. Liked that he just held her. Ten years ago she'd ached for him to do that. When she'd been so lonely…

'How many months pregnant were you when you lost the baby?'

'Seven.' She swallowed, struggling to get the words out. 'It was late. Very late.'

Another soft kiss on her hair. She wasn't in any doubt this time. Seb's arms had tightened around her and he'd kissed her. *Which meant he didn't blame her for getting pregnant.*

Everyone else had seemed to blame her—except Eliana, who'd been kind. And they'd made plans for the future. Worked out ways she could continue to study. Talked about careers that combined well with motherhood.

The only time Eliana had been cross with her was when she'd refused to make an effort to contact the baby's father to say she was pregnant.

Marianne balled the handkerchief tightly up against the whisky tumbler. 'I'm sorry I didn't tell you.'

She took another sip of whisky. It was lovely the way it burnt a trail down her throat. Warming. Gently soothing. Like Seb's fingers moving in small circles at the nape of her neck.

'Did you try?'

She shook her head. 'At first I thought you'd come and find me. Then I imagined you'd had an accident. Amnesia maybe. You read about that sometimes. In books.'

Silence.

'Then I was too angry.'

'At what point did you find out I'd lied about who I was?'

Marianne registered his use of the word 'lie' and it was like a soothing balm.

'That was later. I didn't know for weeks.' She took another sip of whisky. 'I didn't understand why you'd left me. I was frightened by so many changes so quickly. Hurt by my mum and dad. Just taking one day at a time.'

Seb reached out and gently pushed back her hair so he could look into her eyes. 'I'm sorry.'

His own eyes were so warm. So incredibly warm. Then he kissed her forehead and tucked her close against him, his chin resting on the top of her head. She could feel him breathing.

'It didn't seem real until I could feel the baby move inside me.' She sipped her drink. 'Little kicks—sometimes she had the hiccups. When I went to my first scan I thought she looked like a kidney bean. Kind of.'

Marianne cradled the tumbler in her hand and looked down at the deep gold colour and the softly melting ice cubes. That scan had been an amazing experience.

She'd gone in a frightened girl and walked out determined to be the best mother she could, whatever the personal cost. She'd seen her baby and she'd loved her. 'Everything was going normally. She was moving about, sucking her thumb.'

Seb planted another soft kiss against her hair. 'And then she stopped moving inside me. I knew something was wrong straight away. Eliana told me not to panic, that babies were sometimes quiet for a while. But we rang the midwife anyway and she said to go to the hospital…as a precaution.'

It had been a long drive into Cambridge. They'd hit all the school traffic and it had been difficult to find a space in the hospital car park.

'They hooked me up to a monitor and tried to find a heartbeat.' Her voice became choked. Maybe this was more information than he needed. Wasn't it enough to know their baby had died?

'The midwife called a doctor and she told me that the machines sometimes played up, so they'd send me for a scan.' She dragged air into her body. 'And after that scan I had a second scan, but it was the same result: "The amniotic fluid around the baby severely reduced" and they could find "no foetal movement".'

Jessica was dead.

Marianne sat up and drank the last of her whisky. Her head felt slightly fuzzy from the alcohol, but that was good.

'They said they'd have to terminate the pregnancy.' 'Terminate'—such a neat word for what had followed. 'So they gave me a labour-inducing injection—'

'You had to give birth?'

His question seemed to have been wrenched from him. 'I was seven months pregnant. Everyone said it would be safer.'

Seb's face seemed to have become two shades paler. She passed him her empty glass to put on the table. 'They let me hold her,' she smiled tremulously, 'when she was born. She was lovely. She had little fingers with tiny, tiny nails.

Completely perfect.' Marianne drew in a shuddering breath. 'But she was dead.'

Her little girl had been so beautiful…and had looked so peaceful.

'Eliana said I should give her a name. So I called her Jessica.'

'Jessica,' he repeated softly.

'It means "God is watching".' Marianne brushed a hand across her face. 'Eliana thought that was nice because God would watch over her now. Keep her safe for me.'

And that was it really. No need to tell him how it had felt to go home without her baby girl. How it had felt to look down at her stomach and not really believe it was empty.

There was no need to tell him any of that because one glance at his face told her that he knew. His eyes were bleak—as though something inside of him had died too.

'They did an autopsy and said they thought she must have been strangled by her umbilical cord because everything else was normal. Just one of those things.'

Seb reached for her and held her tight against him. His warmth wrapped about her and she lay quietly against his chest. This would have helped her. Back then. Eliana had been good, but she'd needed Seb.

She felt so tired.

'About three weeks after that I saw a photograph of you with your fiancée.'

With his arms about her that didn't seem so difficult to say. Didn't hurt so much.

'That's how you discovered who I was?' he asked, speaking into her hair.

Marianne nodded. She felt so tired and the effect of the whisky was biting. 'I hated you then,' she said, her words blurred and indistinct. 'That's why I can't do this. Can't let you hurt me again.'

Her eyelids were so heavy. And her arms and legs were heavy. Everything heavy and she was so, so sleepy.

'Marianne?'

She heard him say her name as though it was muffled.

'Sweetheart, come on.'

Marianne knew that she ought to answer. Say something to him. But she was so tired.

'Let's get you to bed.'

She felt him pull her jumper over her head and

tried to be helpful. Then he picked her up and she felt as if she were flying.

Seb laid Marianne on his bed and stepped back to look at her. Her fine blonde hair was splayed out across his pillow, her fingers still loosely clutching his handkerchief. The whisky and the past had hit her with a vengeance.

He laid her jumper at the end of the bed and wondered whether he should do anything to make her more comfortable, though she looked peaceful enough. Maybe her shoes? Seb eased off both flat pumps without her stirring, then walked across to his dressing room to fetch a light duvet.

No wonder she hated him. His opinion of himself had taken a dive. She'd been eighteen and a virgin when he'd met her.

Seb walked back through to his bedroom, opened out the duvet and spread it across the top of her. Then he lightly brushed her hair off her face. Every instinct he had was urging him to lie down beside her, but he didn't have the right to do that.

She'd told him she didn't want him to kiss her. That she couldn't allow him to hurt her again.

That single phrase would probably stay with him for ever. He'd never wanted to hurt her. *Never*. But what he'd done could have destroyed her.

And what if Jessica had lived? Their daughter? Seb ran a hand across his chin. He didn't honestly know the answer to that. He liked to think it would have given him the moral courage to stand his ground. Marry her anyway. However unhappy, his father would never have objected so strongly that he'd have seen the crown pass to anyone other than his son.

But…

At nineteen he hadn't had the confidence to challenge the accepted way of doing things. He'd been brought up to believe that with great blessings there came great responsibilities. Marrying someone who had the background and training to become the princess of Andovaria was his God-given responsibility.

He'd married Amelie. Because everyone around him had said it was the right thing to do. The best thing for Andovaria.

But everyone had been wrong. The constitutional crisis they'd feared would happen if he'd married Marianne had happened anyway.

Seb looked down at Marianne sleeping peacefully. He'd loved to watch her sleeping—the slow rise and fall of her breasts, her softly parted lips and the tiny murmur she made as she rolled over. He walked over to dim the lights and walked back out to the sitting room. It seemed intrusive to watch her now.

Damn, but his head ached.

On the rare occasions when he'd allowed himself to think about Marianne he'd thought about her in terms of something he'd had to give up. He'd not really thought about the consequences his decision would have had on her life. There were no acceptable excuses for that.

Seb lay down on the sofa and let his head lean back on the armrest. She'd said she'd hated him then. She must have—but *still* she hadn't sold her story to the papers. Told no one it seemed. Even though she'd hated him…

And they'd made a baby together. Seb drew his hand across his face again, feeling the stubble on his chin. *Dear God*, if he'd known about her pregnancy, would he still have let her down?

Seb pulled his hand across his face again. He'd left Marianne alone. He should have been there to comfort her when their baby died. At the very least he should have made sure she could contact **him** if...

He swore softly. He'd never dreamt Marianne might be pregnant. They'd been so careful. Every time. *Except the first time.*

Not that time because their hormones had over-taken them and they were lovers before they'd known it was a possibility they might be.

Seb pulled himself to his feet and paced about the room restlessly. He couldn't bear thinking of how she must have felt when she saw the pictures of his engagement to Amelie. How betrayed.

But what should he do now? What did he *want* now? By kissing her in view of the security cameras he'd forced himself to make a decision. Marianne would be looked on by his staff as either his girlfriend and their potential princess, or as his lover. There was no middle ground.

Seb walked over to the drinks table and poured himself a second whisky, much larger than the first. Things had changed in the last decade. Crown Prince Frederik of Denmark had married for love. As had Crown Prince Felipe of Spain and Crown Prince Haakon of Norway. In fact, Haakon had married a single mother called Mette-Marit and the whole country had rejoiced with them.

A relationship with Marianne *was* now possible in a way that it simply hadn't been ten years ago.

He sat back down on the sofa, elbows resting on his knees with his glass cradled between his hands. And it was his decision entirely now. No one had to sanction or ratify his marriage.

But what he couldn't do was make a second mistake. The end of his marriage was still a contentious issue with many even though it had been annulled on the grounds that it 'never was a marriage'. If there'd been children it would probably have been impossible for them to separate without doing irreparable damage to the monarchy.

He had to be sure that his next bride would be able to fulfil her role as his consort. She'd have to learn the Alemannic dialect favoured in his principality. Embrace the Lutheran religion of his country, publicly at least. Forgo the rights to her children in the event of marriage breakdown…

Difficult, very difficult things to ask of a modern career woman who hadn't been brought up to expect these demands.

But not impossible. Not if she loved him enough.

Seb stood up and pushed open the door of his bedroom and looked at Marianne. Still asleep. He didn't know whether she'd want those things. Whether he'd hurt her so deeply she'd never be able to forgive him.

He still wasn't even sure what he wanted from their relationship. People changed a lot in ten years. *He'd* changed. Marianne would have too.

But what he did know was that he didn't want her to walk out of his life.

CHAPTER NINE

MARIANNE opened her eyes and knew immediately that she wasn't where she should be. Everything about the enormous bedroom was unfamiliar and it didn't take many more moments to realise where she must be.

She groaned and put her hands over her eyes as though it would block out the reality of it. There were voices in the next-door room, too—which must have been what had woken her. Marianne lay quietly, trying to make out what was being said, scarcely daring to move in case she drew attention to herself. Being discovered in Seb's bed, albeit fully clothed, was going to be a hundred times worse than being caught on a security camera kissing him.

Because she *had* kissed him. She remembered that. And she remembered how difficult it had been to tell him she couldn't let him hurt her again. Even harder to explain the reason why.

A tiny rap on the door and Seb's voice startled her. 'Breakfast.'

Breakfast?

Marianne sat up in bed and clutched at the duvet.

'Marianne?'

It was one of those moments when she wondered whether the best course of action would be to lie back down and put a pillow over her head, but as the door began to open the ostrich manoeuvre was obviously no longer an option.

Seb stood in the doorway, still in the clothes he'd worn last night, looking completely relaxed and unbelievably sexy with the dark stubble on his chin. A real 'morning-after-the-night-before' look. 'Breakfast is on its way.'

'F-for me?'

'Of course for you. What do you want to drink? Tea or coffee?'

Marianne tried to think, but it was difficult. This whole experience had all the bizarre elements of a nightmare. She wasn't even quite sure how she came to be here. Not entirely. She remembered the whisky and the crying…and the way Seb had held her…

She brushed her hair out of her eyes.

'What time is it?'

'Eight.' He walked across and sat on the edge of her bed. *His bed*. 'How are you feeling?'

'Fine.' Marianne swallowed. Having him sit so close to her made her entire nervous system feel as if it was dancing. She tucked her hair behind her ears and struggled to appear as though unexpectedly waking in a gorgeous man's bed was something she could take in her stride. 'I'm sorry, I must have fallen asleep. Did I?'

For a moment he looked as if he might reach out and touch her and her stomach rolled over in fear and excitement. 'You went out like a light.'

'Wh-where did you sleep?'

'On the sofa.'

He'd slept on the *sofa*? Grief, but this was embarrassing. Six feet three inches of athletic male squeezed on a small sofa simply because she couldn't hold her alcohol or manage her emotions. 'I'm sorry.'

'Don't be. That was quite a conversation. Come and have some breakfast.' He stood up and walked back towards the door, stopping to ask again, 'Tea or coffee?'

Marianne was left feeling slightly open-mouthed. How could he say *'That was quite a conversation'* and *'Come and have some breakfast'* in the same breath? Last night she'd told him they'd created a baby together and that their baby had died. Didn't he have anything to say about that?

'Marianne?'

'Tea.' She blinked hard. 'I'll have tea.'

Seb nodded and shut the door. Marianne flung back the duvet, setting her bare feet down on the thick carpet. The sooner she got herself out of here and back where she ought to be the better.

She'd always be glad she'd told him about Jessica—and, in a curious way, she felt that some of the burden of it had been lifted. But she wished she hadn't cried all over him. And she really wished she hadn't fallen asleep up here. That was just embarrassing.

Marianne put a hand to her head and groaned silently as she thought a little more about it. He must have carried her into his bedroom because she sure as hell couldn't remember walking there.

She padded round the other side of the bed and swore as she banged her shin on the edge of it. If she could just find her shoes…

She'd got no recollection of having taken them off, which must mean Seb had done that too. Thank goodness he'd stopped at her shoes. If she'd woken up in nothing but her lacy knickers she'd have died of mortification.

But she still needed to ask him where he'd put them. They were nowhere she could see.

Marianne ran urgent fingers through her hair and smoothed out her long cotton skirt, then stood with her hand on the door handle for a moment while she tried to whip up the courage to walk out there.

Just do it. How difficult could it be? Seb clearly wasn't uncomfortable with her being here, so she just had to walk out there and ask him where he'd put her shoes.

The sooner she did it, the sooner she could escape back to the guest wing—hopefully before too many of the castle security staff were out and about.

She pushed open the door.

Seb looked up from the newspaper he was reading and smiled at her.

Oh, God. Why did this feel so difficult? And why did he have to look so sexy in the morning? 'I can't seem to find my shoes,' she mumbled.

'I might have left them in the dressing room when I went to get myself a duvet last night. Come and have your tea, it's getting cold.'

Marianne looked over her shoulder in the hope she'd see where his dressing room was located. 'Sh-shouldn't I hurry away before anyone knows I'm here?'

'Why?'

Why? It all seemed perfectly clear to her. 'Because someone will see me.'

'The paparazzi have never managed to get a photograph of me here. Poltenbrunn Castle is quite private—'

'Apart from the cameras and the security guards,' she slipped in drily.

'Apart from that,' Seb agreed, a glint of humour lighting his dark eyes. 'Come and drink your tea.'

He was sitting at a small table next to open French doors. Last night she hadn't noticed either the doors or the table. She padded across the luxurious and totally impractical cream carpet.

Without her shoes she felt at a complete disadvantage. 'D-do you always have breakfast here?'

'Usually.'

As she sat down he folded up his newspaper and put it to one side. And she wished he hadn't. It made this whole breakfast thing feel intimate and she didn't think she could cope with that.

She didn't want to be 'intimate'. The whole point of telling him about Jessica was to make sure he understood why she couldn't give in to…whatever it was that kept flaring between them. And to make sure he let her walk away easily, with her self-respect intact—and preferably without the entire staff of Poltenbrunn Castle whispering behind their hands.

'How are you going to get me out of here?'

He picked up his coffee. 'I was thinking we might ambush the person who delivers our breakfast and then you could escape down the trellis in her clothes.'

'Wh…'

His mouth twitched and his dark eyes were laughing over the top of his coffee-cup. 'I'm joking. I suggest we use the same way we came in.'

'But, I don't …'

Marianne stopped speaking as the door to his private rooms opened and a uniformed member of staff wheeled in a trolley. She turned back to look at him, expecting to see... Well, she wasn't sure what she was expecting, but it wasn't to see him calmly putting his coffee-cup back down on the table.

'I wasn't sure what you'd want for breakfast so I asked for a selection,' he said, exactly as if having breakfast with a women in his private rooms was a normal occurrence.

Which, of course, it might be for all she knew. Even discounting fifty per cent of what she'd read over the last few years, Seb wasn't a hermit and his opportunities were broader than most. From her perspective that made this whole thing so much worse. She just wanted to wake up again and find this had been a bad dream.

She answered the woman's rapid German in a faltering version of her own, settling on toast for no other reason than she was too embarrassed to look properly.

Every instinct was encouraging her to bury her face in her hands and cover her head with the starched white tablecloth. She felt exactly as she had when her father had caught her caught her kissing her first boyfriend after the school disco.

Seb appeared entirely comfortable with this whole situation. He made his own selection from the breakfast trays, talked easily and oozed sophisticated charm.

'Everyone will think I've slept here,' Marianne said as soon as the door closed behind the maid.

Seb picked up his coffee again. 'You did.'

'But I'd prefer it if everyone didn't know that. They'll think you and I…'

Marianne trailed off helplessly. Seb knew perfectly well what conclusions his staff would leap to. He didn't need her to spell it out.

'Everyone who works here understands the need to be discreet.'

Which wasn't the point! 'That doesn't mean they aren't thinking it, only that they won't say it.'

He set his coffee-cup down. 'I think you may be surprised what they're thinking. I've never brought any of my female friends to Poltenbrunn.'

She looked across at him, a spark of anger in her expressive eyes. 'That's not the point. I've got my professional reputation to look after. I don't want my colleagues thinking that you and I are…' She picked up her knife and smeared butter across her toast.

Again that gleam of amusement. Sudden and unexpected. 'Are?'

Marianne put her knife down with a clatter. 'Lovers. All right? I've said it. Lovers. I don't want people thinking that I'm your lover.'

'Why?'

Her mouth moved wordlessly and then she said, 'Been there, done that, don't intend to do it again.' She picked up her toast as though she was going to take a bite, but then put it back down again. 'In my world, Seb, it's not about whether or not you're considered "suitable" or who your parents are—'

'I don't believe that.'

'And how would you know? Your entire experience of real life comes down to the five weeks you spent with me. That doesn't exactly make you an expert on what "normal" people do or how "normal" people plan their lives.'

Seb loved the way she did that. One moment she was delightfully confused, the next she was fiery and opinionated. 'So you're saying,' he said mildly, 'that your parents will be equally happy if you marry the drug-addict son of a convicted murderer as opposed to the lawyer son of their local doctor?'

'That's extreme and you know it.'

He shook his head. 'My life is extreme. I can't afford to act without some thought.'

'How romantic!'

Seb smiled again. She looked the way he imagined a ruffled pigeon might. 'No, it's not romantic. The only time I've been free to do exactly as I wished was when I was with you. And that's why you're here.'

As he said the words a *frisson* of awareness passed between them. It always did whenever they allowed themselves to remember what they'd once had together. Marianne's eyes fell away and she looked down, apparently fascinated by the toast on her plate.

Seb took a deep breath. This was it. This was the point at which he needed to try and put words on all the complicated thoughts he'd sat up all night thinking. And honestly, it scared the hell out of him. 'How do you feel about me?'

Her eyes flicked up. 'I don't really know you any more.'

'Perhaps not. But I still need to know how you feel about me.' He kept watching her, hoping, expecting her to say she still cared about him. 'Marianne, it's important.'

'Why?'

His mouth twisted into a wry smile. He should have known that this more mature and confident Marianne would throw his question back at him.

'Because I kissed you,' he said simply.

'I don't understand.'

Seb pushed his chair back and stood up. He'd feel better on his feet. It was how he'd done most of his thinking anyway, pacing up and down the floor. Somehow she'd managed to turn the tables on him. When he'd planned this conversation in his head it had run along completely different lines.

He wasn't good at saying how he felt. He hadn't had a great deal of practice—and he wasn't sure what words to use. Where to start. How you even began to unpack all the thought processes that had led him to this point.

'I kissed you,' he repeated, his hand rubbing the back of his neck, 'when I didn't want to.'

He knew he'd made a mistake when a frown snapped across her forehead.

'Didn't mean to,' he corrected swiftly. 'I kissed you when I didn't mean to. I spoke to you in Amiens when I didn't mean to. I travelled with you to Paris when I shouldn't have.' Seb wasn't sure this was going at all well. Marianne was still staring at him as though he'd gone completely mad.

'What I'm trying to say…is that you…affect me.' He cringed at such an out dated choice of word. It had come out of nowhere. *Affect* me. What was the matter with him? He was good with women. Spent a lot of time with lots of very beautiful women and none of them made him feel so tongue-tied and awkward.

He was trying to say that he was reaching out, for only the second time in his adult life, for what he really wanted. And both times he'd been reaching for her.

'I affect you?' she said with a slight lift of her right eyebrow.

He blew out the breath that he'd been holding in one short burst. *Yes, she affected him.* Deeply and profoundly. And she shouldn't.

Seb looked at Marianne with one bare foot crossed on top of the other, her skirt clearly showing the signs of having been slept in, no make-up on and hair that only just merited the description tousled rather than tangled.

She really *shouldn't* affect him. Only she did. He'd spent his entire life surrounded by women with easy access to haute couture and all the beauty treatments money could buy—but not one of them had made him *feel* so much.

Just looking at her made him want to re-think his day. Meetings with his mother, his head groom, the estate manager and the diplomatic reception no longer seemed particularly pressing. Marianne made him want to peel her T-shirt away from her incredible body and slip her skirt down and over her hips. He wanted to kiss a trail up the side of her neck and feel her breasts heavy in his hands.

Seb swallowed painfully. *He wanted far more than that.* He wanted her in his bed and completely certain she was going to stay there. How did you tell someone that they were filling your senses in a way that defied all logic? From the first time he'd seen her and every time since. When he was with her he forgot everything except that he wanted her.

And it wasn't merely lust. He liked her.

Genuinely liked being with her. He wanted to talk to her and know all the thoughts that were going on behind her intelligent eyes.

But he couldn't ask her to be his long-term lover—because she'd already told him she wouldn't be happy. Didn't want that.

Which left marriage. And it was too soon in their relationship to make that kind of a decision. In all fairness to her, he had to make it clear what a life with him would be like….

Marianne stood up, leaving her half-eaten toast on her plate and her tea untouched. 'I think I'd better find my shoes,' she said quietly. 'I assume your dressing room is through there?'

He must have nodded because she walked through to his bedroom and disappeared out of sight. He felt as though something incredibly precious was falling through his fingers and he didn't know how to stop it.

Seb pulled a shaking hand through his hair and tried to focus on what had seemed such a sensible proposition last night. He would 'court' her, sensibly and openly. She'd have a chance to see what being royal entailed and they could monitor the public's reaction to her.

As privately as possible, with no breath of a scandal, they could see where this connection would take them. See whether she'd be a suitable princess of Andovaria. It was reasonable, balanced and adult.

But that wasn't romantic. He couldn't give her that. He couldn't simply follow his heart and propose to her now. He had a responsibility to his country….

'What I'm trying to say,' he said as soon as she reappeared with her jumper held protectively in front of her and her shoes on her feet, 'is that I'm still attracted to you.'

'I'm understanding you perfectly.' Her voice was crisp and dry, clearly misinterpreting what he was trying to say.

'Marianne—'

'Stop it! Just stop it!' Her brown eyes darted a mixture of anger and hurt. 'This might be a new experience for you, Your Serene Highness, but you've just met someone you can't buy and who's not starry-eyed that you're a prince. What I gave you was a gift. My gift to you because I loved you and I wanted to be with you.'

She shook her head in apparent disbelief and

drew in one long, shaky breath. 'I'm sure you'll find someone who'll *affect* you equally and who won't mind that they're not *suitable* for anything more permanent. After all, don't want to taint the stock line, do we?'

'That's not what I meant.'

Marianne brushed past him. She felt as though she'd been violated. It hurt that someone she'd loved so deeply as Seb could treat her as a commodity. Little more than a body. How could he believe she'd settle for so little, a tiny piece of his life?

And she'd told him she couldn't become his lover. 'I know exactly what you meant.'

'No, you don't.' Seb caught her by the top of her arms, holding her with just enough strength to stop her trajectory. 'I'm trying to tell you that I want you in my life.'

'And I'm telling you I'm not interested.'

Seb's hands refused to let her go. 'You're not hearing me.' His eyes seemed to pin her to the floor. 'I'd like you to get to know me again. Think about what it would be like to be a princess.'

Marianne went limp and her eyes searched his for some explanation of what he'd said. His words pooled into silence. Unexpected. Totally, totally unexpected.

It hadn't been a question, more a statement of fact. And it made no *sense*. At least not to her.

Sure that she wasn't going anywhere Seb released her arms. He eased a hand round the back of his neck. 'That's what I want,' he said more quietly.

Seb seemed to be waiting for her reaction, but she wasn't sure what she was supposed to be reacting to. It could almost have been an academic question for the amount of emotion he'd put into it.

Not love. He hadn't said he loved her. Just that he wanted her to get to know him and *think* about how she felt about being a princess. Did that mean he wanted her to think about being *his* princess? His *wife*?

Or just to think about what it would be like and understand why she couldn't be?

Marianne started to speak and then decided she couldn't.

'What do you think?' Seb asked, watching her face closely.

She frowned. 'I think I don't understand the

question. Has this got something to do with Jessica?'

'No. Yes.' He pulled a hand through his hair. 'In a way. Maybe.'

'That's clear.'

Seb reached out to take hold of her hand and she let him take it. She'd never seen him like this. Even as a teenager he'd had an aura of confidence about him. It was probably what had attracted her to him in the first place.

'I've sat up all night thinking about you.' His voice was thick and husky, laced with deep emotion. 'About Jessica. About what my life could have been like...'

'If she'd lived?'

'Not exactly, but yes.'

Marianne frowned. This felt rather like the verbal equivalent of walking through fog and, all of a sudden, she'd had enough. 'Seb, I'm not understanding any of this.' She rubbed at her arm, trying to get some life back into limbs that suddenly felt cold and heavy. 'Are you asking me to marry you because you somehow think that'll be a kind of reparation for what happened with Jessica?' It didn't matter whether she was making a complete fool of herself. She just wanted to know. 'If so, you don't have to worry. I'm doing just fine.'

Not entirely true, but true enough. She was surviving—and she'd made a fulfilling and interesting life for herself. In many ways it was good. She lifted her chin and met his dark eyes. 'I didn't tell you about her because I wanted you to feel guilty. Certainly not because I wanted you to feel sorry for me.'

His fingers moved across the back of her hand. It was an incredibly tender gesture.

She watched a muscle pulse in the side of his cheek; saw him searching for the words. 'I know that.'

'I told you about her because she was your baby, too. And because I want you to understand why I can't have another affair with you. I'm not strong enough.'

Seb shook his head. 'I'm not asking you to do that.' His smile twisted. 'Come and sit back down.'

'Seb,' she began wearily, but in the end it seemed easier to do what he wanted.

He led her back to the breakfast table and waited until she'd sat back down.

'Shall I call for some fresh tea?'

'No.' *Just tell me what you want from me.* It was a miracle she'd not said that aloud.

Seb sat himself opposite. She heard his intake of breath and waited for him to speak. It had almost reached the point where she didn't much care what he said as long as he said something. Her nerves were stretched so far she thought they might snap.

'I married Amelie—' he began slowly.

'I know. I saw your wedding pictures.'

He ignored her, focused on whatever it was he wanted to tell her. 'Because her father is the Archduke of Saxe-Broden and he was a close friend of my father. Amelie was—is,' he corrected himself, 'a very beautiful woman. She's intelligent, speaks five languages, is used to moving in royal circles and had no breath of scandal attached to her.'

'She sounds perfect.' Marianne bowed her head so Seb couldn't see how much his words were hurting her.

'That's what my parents thought. And the people of Andovaria. They loved her. It was what they wanted—the young prince in his castle bringing home his virginal princess—and our popularity soared. Which was *exactly* what my father had hoped for when he'd brokered the marriage.'

Marianne swallowed hard. She knew this. Knew all this. When she'd said she'd seen the photographs, she'd really meant she'd seen them. The horse-drawn carriage pulled by six perfectly matched white horses. The streets filled with bunting and cheering crowds.

'And, I suppose, the truth was I didn't much care who I married if I couldn't have you.'

She looked up at that. Her eyes shimmering with tears she would not let fall.

'You were young, English, with no aristocratic connections. No prince in Europe had ever had such a bride. And we were already lovers…'

'Because I loved you,' she said through a throat that felt tight and constricted. She didn't want to hear this.

'Because you loved me,' Seb repeated softly. 'But we'd only had five weeks together. So little time. And to marry you would have been to ask my parents to go against everything they knew or had any experience of.

'Everything my father did as the sovereign prince was designed to keep Andovaria a monarchy and to keep it strong. There were voices of dissent even then—people who have a different vision for Andovaria in the twenty-first century.'

Everything Seb said seemed to have a hateful logic. Amelie had been an inspired choice. The fairy-tale princess.

'But marrying Amelie was difficult. We'd only met a handful of times before our engagement was officially announced and I scarcely knew anything about her other than that she'd been groomed to fill the kind of position I had to offer.'

Marianne nodded because she did understand. It was easy to imagine the pressure he'd been under to conform.

'But I loved you—and I should never have done it. I remember standing in here on my wedding day, dressed in my ceremonial uniform, wondering what you were doing.'

Marianne gripped her hands together in her lap. Hard.

'Hoping you were happy. Hoping I was doing the right thing, but knowing it was too late to do anything else.'

He stopped speaking. The silence sat between them.

'But Amelie is also a quiet and very private person,' Seb continued suddenly. 'She hated pretty much everything that being the Princess of Andovaria entails. She doesn't like talking to strangers, giving speeches, walking into a room and have people watch her...'

Marianne looked up.

'She found the state dinners an ordeal. She hated being photographed and having her clothes criticised. Hated having bodyguards with her whenever she left the castle.

'And she didn't love me. Between ourselves we knew very early on that our marriage wasn't going to work. We were married for five and a half years, but for five of those we were actively working towards our very amicable separation.'

He stood up abruptly and walked out onto the narrow balcony. Marianne turned in her chair so she could see him more clearly. Seb claimed not to have loved Amelie, but the failure of his marriage clearly bothered him. Offended him deeply.

'What's Amelie doing now?'

Seb turned his head slightly. 'She's living in the States. Studying for the degree she always wanted.'

'Happy?'

He nodded. 'She seems to be.'

'But you're not?' Marianne asked hesitantly.

His shoulder muscles bunched beneath the fine wool of his jumper. 'I feel I've failed. The divorce rate in Andovaria is the lowest in Europe. The people here are traditional and hold traditional family values'.

He turned. 'If I marry again—and I have to—there'll be no possibility of divorce or a second annulment. When I marry it has to be for life.'

The tell-tale muscle in the corner of his cheek pulsed. Marianne watched both it, and him.

'That's why I'm saying you need to think about what it would be like to be the Princess of Andovaria.'

Light burst in Marianne's head like fireworks.

'I want to get to know you and for you to know me, but it's not that simple. As soon as the Press get wind of the fact that we're seeing each other your life will be completely different. The paparazzi will swoop on your family and friends and their lives will change too.'

He moved back into the room. 'Whether or not we ultimately decide to marry, you'll always be known as a former girlfriend of the Prince of Andovaria. Your face will be recognised and your life interesting to people you've never met.'

Marianne swallowed. Yesterday she'd been sure where her life was going; today everything seemed to be shifting about.

'It's not easy. Isabelle was born to it and she seems to hate every moment. Amelie was hurt by it.' His smile twisted. 'I don't want you to answer me now. I want you to think about it. Really think about whether you would be happy living with cameras aimed at you all the time, knowing that video tapes can be slowed down and analysed so your words can be lip-read.

'Think about the effect it would have on your career. About never being able to express an opinion that might be construed as political.'

Marianne tucked her hair behind her ears. She was trying so hard to concentrate on what he was saying. 'So,' she said slowly, 'you're asking to *date* me?'

'With a view to marriage. Perhaps. If we feel you would…'

'Be suitable.' Marianne finished his sentence for him. She felt as if he'd reached inside her and had squeezed her heart. At eighteen that had been her dream. She'd loved him. Wanted desperately to spend her life with him…

But it hadn't been possible. In London he'd said…Marianne frowned. 'I don't understand what's changed. Why is it now possible for me to marry you when it wasn't before?'

There was a brief tap on the outside door. Seb glanced over at it. 'That'll be Alois wanting to discuss today's schedule.'

He walked over to the door and spoke quietly. Marianne didn't try to hear what he was saying. Her mind was a complete mess. She sat in stupefied silence.

Seb shut the door and smiled at her as though he could see what she was feeling. 'What's changed is that princes are now able to marry for love. Denmark, Spain, Norway…even your own country. And in each case the marriage has somehow brought the monarchy more popularity. Made it more accessible to the people. But it's a huge lifestyle change and you'd have to want to embrace those changes as much as me.'

'Wouldn't there be a scandal if it was discovered I'd been pregnant with your baby when you married Amelie?'

'Yes.' He couldn't lie to her. There would be an immense scandal. Isabelle's behaviour was offending a huge swathe of Andovaria and he honestly doubted whether public opinion would allow him to marry a woman who'd been his lover. Particularly if they suspected his relationship with her might have been a contributory factor in the breakdown of his fledgling marriage.

Seb smiled at her. 'I think if that kind of information was out there it would have surfaced by now. Certainly when I separated from Amelie.'

He could tell she was still doubtful. Not particularly surprising since she'd grown up with salacious stories about the British royal family in the Press on a nearly daily basis.

'I would trust Nick with my life. And if Beth had wanted to sell our story she could have done it by now.'

'She wouldn't!'

'Then I think we can stop worrying about it. It's more important you take the time to think about what marriage to me would be like. Take as much time as you need to be sure. We'll spend some time together. Talk.'

But not become lovers.

'And we'll try and keep our friendship a secret from the Press. There's no point stirring up speculation unless we intend to marry in due course. And we're not going to know that for a while.'

Marianne nodded and got to her feet. 'I—I don't know. It's difficult and I…'

His hands moved to cradle her face and he looked down into her eyes. He was so close she could see the tiny flecks of amber, feel his breath on her skin. 'I need you to think about it because I think I'm falling in love with you again,' he said simply.

There was a brief moment of shivering delight when she knew he was going to kiss her, before his mouth fastened on hers. His kiss was warm, persuasive and so, so unbelievably sexy. And it was a kiss unlike any she'd ever known. It was honest and real and it touched the very essence of who she was.

Her jumper fell to the ground and she raised a shaking hand to feel the rough bristles on his chin. Seb might be falling in love with her all over again, but she'd already fallen. And she'd fallen hard—ten years ago—with no prospect of pulling back.

But what he was asking…scared her.

CHAPTER TEN

TWENTY-FOUR hours later and Marianne still wasn't sure of her decision. Every time she thought she'd decided to take a chance on what she felt for Seb she remembered how desperately hurt she'd been by him. How broken.

And he was offering no guarantees about their having a long term future together even now. Couldn't. What he was offering her was simply the *possibility* of one.

Marianne left the formal parterre and headed directly for the pavilion, loving the feel of the mid-morning sun on her skin after the chill of the keep.

She glanced down at her watch. Actually, she'd had more than twenty-four hours to make her decision. Seb's oh-so-disciplined private secretary had escorted her back to the guest wing at five minutes to nine, which meant she'd had twenty-five hours and forty-

nine minutes to reach some kind of a conclusion.

What Seb was suggesting would change her
life. Irrevocably. She didn't know if she was
ready for what that would mean. How could she
ever really know what it was like to live the life
of a princess, or a potential princess, until she
was actually doing it? And by then it would be
too late to turn back.

Marianne tucked herself into a corner of the
pavilion, slipping off her shoes and stretching her
legs out along the cushioned seating. It was nice
up here. It didn't have the fairy-tale grandeur of
Seb's 'postcard' view, but she loved the revolving
table in the pavilion that made her think of a noisy
family eating out-of-doors and the sweeping lawn
that was made for children to play on.

It made her believe it might be possible to
carve herself a life here with Seb. She wanted it
to be possible because she loved him. Still.

But…it was difficult.

If they'd had the same conversation a decade
ago she wouldn't have thought about it for a
moment. She'd have jumped at the chance to be
with him whatever the sacrifices involved.

Only now she was older. Had seen more, understood more. Marianne opened the flap of her small rucksack and pulled out her flask of coffee. She loved Seb and wanted to be with him, but it wasn't that simple.

It was like marrying a man who had children from a previous relationship; the children were part of the package and you couldn't ignore them. Seb was the Sovereign Prince of Andovaria and, like it or not, he came as a package. Seb *and* Andovaria.

And it wasn't even merely a question of embracing a new country; it was having to live by a completely different set of rules.

How would it feel to know you were considered important simply because you'd happened to fall in love with and marry a prince? To have people worry about whether they should call you ma'am or Serene Highness?

To have no real friends?

How did that feel? Never to be completely sure whether people genuinely liked you—or merely the status you brought them by knowing you?

What did it feel like to be hounded by the

Press? To be Princess Isabelle? To be pursued by the paparazzi—who knew that a bad photograph of you had more market value than a good one? What did that feel like, day after day?

Could she cope with a future where everything she wore, everything she said, would all be analysed and criticised...

Was she ready for that?

Honestly, she didn't think she was. The prospect terrified her. But when she thought of the alternative...leaving Seb...

Marianne unscrewed the top of her flask and carefully poured herself a coffee. She wasn't sure she could do that either. She sat back into the corner, her hands cradled round the flask-lid mug, her head whirring with all the thinking.

When she was with him she forgot he was a prince. Forgot everything except how it felt to be with him, to be able to touch him, hold him.

Have him hold her.

She wanted that.

A shadow fell across the revolving table, giving her a few seconds warning that she was about to be joined, before Seb stepped inside the pavilion. He was dressed in a sharply cut black suit, black tie and crisp white shirt. Formal. Intimidating. And spectacularly attractive.

Marianne took a moment to respond to him being there—and when she did it was with a jerk. She flicked her legs to the ground and spilt a little of her coffee on her skirt as she did so. 'I thought you'd gone,' she said, foolishly. 'I heard a helicopter.'

'Yes, I'm about to go. I told them to wait.'

'Oh.'

'I saw you walk up here.'

Unaccountably shy, Marianne looked away—using the need to place her coffee back down on the table as an excuse. Then she pulled the wrap-over on her ecru linen skirt in place and traced a finger over the coffee stain.

'Where are you going?'

'There's been a serious train crash on the border between Andovaria and Switzerland,' Seb said, sitting next to her.

'No!'

'I'm flying in to see if I can help get things moving a little quicker.'

'Are many people hurt?' she asked, shocked.

He nodded. 'The local hospitals are expecting

to be overstretched. So far thirty people are known to have been seriously injured, but they're still pulling people from the wreckage.'

'Any dead?'

'Not yet.' He looked across at her. 'I find this kind of thing difficult to deal with.'

Marianne reached out a hand and laid it across his. She did it without thinking, merely intending to comfort. His fingers closed round hers and held her hand firmly.

'What I hate the most is that when I arrive you can see people look at me and think "Great, now he'll get things sorted" and I know there's nothing I can do that isn't already being done.'

His forefinger moved against the palm of her hand. 'I feel helpless.'

Marianne said nothing. She sat and watched his finger move rhythmically over her skin.

'Five years ago there was a fairly serious train accident,' Seb continued, 'and a child was pinned in one of the carriages. I climbed in to talk to him while the rescue services were getting organised. They had to cut him out.'

'Oh, Seb.'

'I'm still haunted by his voice pleading with me not to leave him.'

'Did he survive?' she asked, her voice sounding husky.

'He lost a leg. Eight years old and he lost a leg.' Seb moved his hand and threaded his fingers through hers. 'Just doesn't seem fair, does it?'

'Better than dying.'

'Yes.' He looked out across the sweeping expanse of lawn and towards the neatly arranged parterre. 'Doesn't seem to let it stop him doing anything. He's quite inspirational. As is his mother.'

His fingers moved again against her hand. 'They'd been going to see friends. Set out that morning expecting to have a pleasant day…'

'Accidents happen,' she said. 'And, even if you can't do as much as you'd like to, at least you're trying to do something. And you can throw your weight about and demand things happen faster. That's good.'

Seb turned back to her and smiled. 'Yes, I can do that.'

The expression in his eyes stopped the air in her lungs.

The pressure on her fingers increased. 'Have you made your decision?'

Had she? She was holding his hand. Wanted to comfort him.

Marianne released her trapped breath on one shaky outpouring. 'Yes. Yes, I have.'

'And will you?'

'Yes.' And it felt as if she'd jumped into a vast vat of fizzing lemonade.

Seb reached out and cradled one cheek in his warm hand, lightly kissing her softly parted lips. They hardly touched and yet Marianne could feel the tremor run through him and she felt a sudden surge of confidence. He might not know it, but she was sure he loved her. Just as he had before.

'You ought to go.'

'Yes.'

'I'd hoped we could have had dinner today,' Seb said, his thumb gently stroking across her cheek, 'but I don't know when I'll be back. It depends what I find when I get there.'

She shook her head. 'It doesn't matter.'

'And Saturday is the annual summer ball.' His eyes seemed to caress her. 'Come.'

'To the ball?'

Seb nodded. 'See what you think of it.'

A shiver of fear passed through her. A royal ball. At the castle. Where people would look at her and wonder who she was.

It was the point of no return—and they both knew it. *Prince Sebastian's girlfriend.*

'I'll send Alois to talk to you. Finalise the arrangements.'

Slowly Marianne nodded.

Seb's mouth curved into a sexy smile and then he leant in for another kiss. This time more certain and his tongue flicked between her lips. That still made her gasp, want more…

'See you Saturday. If not before.' His lips pressed warm against her forehead. Then he stood up and briskly walked back down towards the castle.

Marianne watched him go, uncertain whether she was relieved to have made the decision or apprehensive about what that decision would mean.

By the time Marianne returned to the guest wing that evening she'd heard more than enough about the annual summer ball. As soon as the invitations had arrived there was very little conversation in the keep office that didn't concern it.

Dr Liebnitz had received an invitation, the professor and his wife, two of the more senior historians on the team, their partners…and herself. No one had quite known what to make of it, since it was apparently unprecedented for any 'staff' member to be invited to what was, essentially, a high-society event.

She shut the door of the Blue Suite and rested her head on it, glad of the solitude. The constant speculation had made her feel awkward. Untruthful—because she'd known exactly what had prompted the Dowager Princess to send those cream invitations.

Marianne slipped her shoes off her feet and padded across to the kettle. What she was less sure of was whether the Dowager Princess knew she'd sent them. How much had Seb told his family? And how much was she allowed to confide in Peter and Eliana?

She placed the kettle in its cradle as a firm knock sounded on the outside door.

'Just coming,' Marianne called out, expecting it to be the professor…or Eliana. 'I'm…' She broke off, stunned to see Alois von Dietrich.

Seb's private secretary gave a professional

smile. 'His Serene Highness asked me to run through tomorrow's arrangements with you as soon as you returned to the guest wing.'

'Oh,' Marianne managed limply. She held the door a little wider. 'You'd better come in.'

'Thank you.'

Marianne tucked her hair behind her ears. 'Would you like something to d-drink?'

'Not for me, thank you.'

She walked over to the chairs by the window and sank down because her legs had begun to feel wobbly. She'd seen Seb's helicopter take off barely twenty minutes after their conversation in the pavilion and yet he seemed to have found time to arrange so much.

'Please sit down.'

What was Alois von Dietrich thinking about her? Did he think what Seb was doing was unwise? Impossible? What did he really think about her having spent the night in his employer's private rooms? Marianne gripped her hands firmly in her lap.

Seb's private secretary took the opposite seat and pulled out his file. 'I've arranged for Gianferro DiBenedetto to bring some of his more wearable designs to the castle at nine o'clock tomorrow.' He looked up. 'Unless there's a designer whose work you prefer, Dr Chambers?'

Her mind spluttered. 'No. Gianferro DiBenedetto will be fine.'

More than fine. He was a phenomenally successful designer; his dresses were fought over by Oscar-nominated actresses. Marianne sat in stunned silence.

'I'm afraid it does need to be early to allow time for any alterations to be made before the evening.' Alois von Dietrich looked up. 'Prince Sebastian also thought that, on this occasion, you'd be more comfortable arriving with your friends, Professor and Mrs Blackwell?'

Marianne's hands clasped and unclasped in her lap. 'Yes. Yes, I would.'

'I suggest, then, that they meet you here at eight o'clock and I'll have someone sent down to escort you through the security.'

'Thank you.'

Alois shut his file. 'I will accompany Signore DiBenedetto to see you in the morning.' He stood up. 'And I wish you a very good night.'

The unmistakable sound of a helicopter flying

close by had Marianne looking anxiously outside the window. 'Is that Prince Sebastian?'

'His Serene Highness doesn't anticipate returning to Poltenbrunn until the morning.'

Marianne looked round. 'Was the crash particularly bad?'

'I believe the total number of injured is now standing at sixty-five and there are three known to have died,' Alois replied. 'An even mix of Swiss and Andovarian nationals.'

It was strange that Seb's private secretary should know more about what was happening in his life than she did. *Different rules.* Did Alois think Seb would have tried to contact her directly if she was important to him? Or did he think it was intrusive of her to want to know?

Marianne stood up. 'Thank you for everything you've done.' And then, with her hand on the door, 'Who is that arriving?'

'Prince Sebastian's youngest sister. With so many photographers outside the castle it wasn't considered safe for Princess Isabelle to arrive by car.'

It was on the tip of her tongue to ask whether Princess Isabelle had arrived alone or whether she'd brought her much older lover with her. She stopped herself just in time.

With the door shut, Marianne placed her hands against her hot cheeks. *This whole experience was so bizarre*. She was going to wear a Gianferro DiBenedetto dress. A dress that would cost more to buy than she earned in a month.

How did Seb imagine she was going to explain that to Eliana?

Perhaps it was time she took her into her confidence? Not about Seb being Jessica's father—that was too private and painful a secret. But about Prince Sebastian wanting to 'date' her. That was incredible enough.

And she needed to tell someone. Put words on what was happening to make it seem believable.

Marianne pulled a jumper from one of the drawers and quickly slipped on her shoes. She let herself out of the Blue Suite and headed out towards the Blackwells' temporary home in the castle grounds.

CHAPTER ELEVEN

IT HAD been a long time since Marianne had needed any help getting dressed, but tonight it seemed she wasn't to be trusted. An army of experts had swooped on her and she was completely transformed.

Gianferro had come especially to see that his elegant bias-cut creation was being shown to the best possible effect, a hairstylist had pulled her hair into a seemingly artless twist and a manicurist had performed a miracle on nails she'd ignored for a whole lifetime.

She looked like a princess, which must have been Seb's intention. And she felt scared. It would have felt better if she'd been able to spend some time with him, but she'd had no contact with Seb since their snatched conversation in the pavilion.

'Hurry up. It's nearly eight o'clock,' Eliana

called out loudly from the next room. 'How long does it take to put on a necklace?'

Marianne drew a shaky breath. She felt exactly as she had when she'd been learning to ice skate and her teacher had told her to let go of the rail. Leaving the bedroom seemed like the hardest thing in the world.

'What do you think?' she asked, stepping into the sitting room.

Eliana's face broke into a smile. 'I think you look incredible.' She walked round Marianne to study her appearance from all angles. 'Very, very beautiful. Don't you, Peter? It's just a more polished version of you, if that makes any sense.'

Marianne ran her hands over the oyster silk. 'This is the weirdest dress. It's got a kind of Lycra smoothing system built into it as part of the actual thing.'

'Is it comfortable?'

Eliana's question surprised a laugh. 'Not particularly. I'm not sure whether I can sit down.'

'Shouldn't think you'll have to.' There was a small tap on the door. 'It's time we were leaving.'

Marianne fingered the heart-shaped locket at her neck. Gianferro had been all for borrowing a diamond drop necklace, but she'd insisted on wearing her own jewellery. She needed to remember what this was all about—and Seb's gift to her was the only thing that would do that.

She was here because she loved him—and because Seb thought he might be falling in love with her. She was here because she needed him. And because she wasn't happy living her life away from him.

'Ready?' the professor asked.

Marianne didn't think she'd ever feel ready, but Alois's organisation was meticulous. His 'someone' was here promptly at eight and would, no doubt, have something scheduled for later.

She was overwhelmingly glad to have Eliana and Peter with her. Glad that they'd taken her news in their stride. Glad they didn't see anything particularly difficult or impossible about it. But *embarrassed* she couldn't confide in them completely.

It made her feel alone. Isolated.

Marianne's fingers strayed once more to the necklace she was wearing. *This mattered.* She couldn't pretend it didn't. Being with Seb mattered. Being 'suitable' mattered.

And this was the first step. Fail here and she would be reduced to nothing more than 'Marianne Chambers, former girlfriend of the Prince of Andovaria'.

Her chin came up and her eyes sparkled against the challenge. She *could* do this. Light strains of something classical wafted towards her. She didn't know what, but it was pleasant and…soothing.

Alois von Dietrich had worked some kind of special magic because their group of three avoided the crush of people moving inexorably towards the ballroom. They were ushered in and through and had nothing left to do but stand in rapt admiration.

The already spectacular room had been transformed into a white bower. There were flowers absolutely everywhere. Large, glossy lilies and twisting rose garlands led the eye towards the wall of open French doors and on into the rose garden beyond.

'Oh, my,' Eliana said in a soft whisper at Marianne's elbow.

Silently, Marianne echoed the sentiment. She felt her fragile confidence falter once again. This was so…*big*. Seb's life was so big.

All around her was the cream of European society. The cost of the dresses the women were wearing alone would probably cancel out Third World debt…and if you factored in their jewels…

Marianne could hear her heart beating, feel the thud as it slammed against her chest cavity. *She didn't want to fail*. She wanted him to love her.

'Their Serene Highnesses Prince Sebastian of Andovaria, the Dowager Princess Arabella…'

Marianne felt as though she'd entered that zone where everything became blurry except one central image. And for her, Seb was that image.

She'd thought she had reached a point where she understood what it meant to be royalty—but this moved her understanding up one notch more. Everyone was looking at him.

Everyone. The eyes of every man and woman, in a room holding more than a thousand people, were on him.

And Seb looked completely unconscious of it. He was used to it…because it was his birthright. Marianne hung back and watched as he led his mother towards the centre of the room. And, like some bizarre version of a Mexican wave, people bowed their heads as they moved through.

Then the entire royal party splintered and they worked the room with practised ease. It was formidable to see. At one point Princess Isabelle stood close enough to be heard and Marianne was amazed she could switch between languages without the slightest hesitation.

'Shouldn't you go and speak to him?' Eliana asked quietly.

Marianne shook her head. 'He's working.'

And that was true. It was a new perspective on what these royal occasions were about. With sudden clarity she recognised how valuable it was that so many of the world's most influential people could be gathered in one place at the same time.

'Dr Chambers?' Alois von Deitrich said quietly. She turned at his voice.

'His Serene Highness Prince Sebastian has asked if you would come this way.'

Marianne felt her heart bounce up into her throat. 'H-has he? Yes. Yes, of course.'

Seb's private secretary seemed to have the ability to cut an effortless swathe through the massed people. Marianne simply tucked in behind him. Her stomach was churning and adrenaline was coursing through her veins.

'Dr Chambers, sir,' Alois said as they drew close enough to be heard.

Marianne managed a small curtsey and looked up into eyes that were wickedly laughing.

Seb leant forward and lightly kissed her cheek, taking the opportunity to whisper, 'I thought we'd agreed you weren't going to do that.'

'It goes against the grain, but I'm behaving well.'

His mouth pulled into a smile. 'I'll treasure the moment.' His hand reached out to take hold of hers. 'Any moment there will be dancing…and I need a partner.'

Marianne looked over her shoulder, worried by who might be watching. 'Should you be holding my hand?'

'Difficult for us to dance together if we don't.' Seb led her towards the centre of the room and then moved to hold her. One hand was pressed in the small of her back and the other kept hold of her hand.

She loved the feel of him. Marianne breathed in and filled her lungs with the smell of his tangy aftershave. 'There's no music.'

'Give them a moment.' And then, as though that had been their cue, the musicians started to play.

Marianne kept looking straight up into Seb's eyes, her feet moving effortlessly. 'What would you have done if I didn't know how to dance?'

'I knew you could,' Seb replied, his eyes alight with mischief.

'How?'

'I was sure that the Under-sixteen Eastern Counties Ballroom Champion would be able to manage a waltz.'

Marianne looked down to a point mid-chest, then back up at his eyes. 'Did I tell you that?'

'Yes.' He spun her round. 'I suddenly remembered it this evening when I was trying to work out how I could get to hold you.'

Her hand trembled. It was what she wanted to hear him say…but she was so confused. For him to dance with her like this was tantamount to making a public announcement. Surely that wasn't what they'd agreed?

'You look beautiful, by the way.'

Marianne's confused eyes flew up to his confidently smiling ones. 'What are you doing?'

'Dancing with you.'

'But why?'

Seb's fingers splayed out against the silk of

her dress and she could feel the warmth of his hand on her skin. It was hard to remember how many hundreds of eyes were watching her at this moment.

'Because I want to.'

'What happened to "dating" me privately? I thought we were going to keep our…friendship a secret while we made sure it was right for both of us.'

'Yes, we were.'

'So, what changed?' Marianne asked.

Seb's hand shifted position on her lower back and she spun round, a mass of tingling sensation. Right now, right here, she didn't care who was watching. Didn't care who thought what. She just wanted to be with him, have him hold her.

He moved in closer and spoke quietly. 'Meet me outside in twenty minutes. By the third window on the left.'

Marianne nodded. She would meet him anywhere. Do anything. Her eyes scanned the side of the ballroom so she was sure where he meant.

'If I hand you over to Alois he'll take you to find your friends.' Then, as the waltz drew to a close, Seb stepped back and smiled.

She knew exactly what that smile meant. It meant 'twenty minutes'. Her stomach was a nervous knot of anticipation—but the fear had gone. There was a new expression in his eyes— one that she recognised.

A tremulous smile played across her mouth. She'd seen it before. In France. It was that expression that had made her fall in love with him.

As Alois led her back through the clusters of people earnestly discussing issues large and small, it became clear that her status had changed. One very public dance with Prince Sebastian and she'd suddenly become interesting.

People wanted to know who she was, what her name was, how she'd met the prince… Alois began by hovering solicitously, but quickly relaxed as Marianne discovered she was quite adept at saying little while still being charming.

She even managed to switch between French, German and English with reasonable alacrity, although she didn't pretend to rival Princess Isabelle's skill. Nevertheless, Alois was impressed.

'Your knowledge of European languages is unusual for an Englishwoman,' he remarked.

Marianne smiled as she heard the grudging

respect in his voice. 'It's not an inability to learn that keeps most of us only speaking English, it's merely that the rest of Europe seems to speak English so well it's difficult to see the need.'

Eliana looked up as Marianne approached. She'd found a seat and was sipping champagne.

'Dr Chambers,' Alois said in farewell, with a curious kind of bow.

'Thank you for returning me to Eliana. I wouldn't have found her without you.' Then as he turned away, Marianne pointed to the seat next to her. 'Is this taken?'

'Peter's only just vacated it,' Eliana replied, looking curiously over the top of her champagne flute.

Marianne gingerly lowered herself down and perched on the edge.

The creases at the edges of Eliana's soft blue eyes deepened. 'So you can sit in that dress,' she remarked.

'Just.'

'Nice dance.'

Marianne looked up and felt an overwhelming desire to laugh. She was happy. Really, genuinely happy. 'What time is it?'

Eliana held out her wrist.

'Oh, goodness,' Marianne said, standing up. 'I've got to go again.'

Her friend's eyes twinkled. 'I see.'

Marianne slid as unobtrusively as possible through the nearest double doors. The light was beginning to fade and the huge torches that had been lit along the length of the terrace had come into their own.

Hundreds of people, it seemed, had decided to take the opportunity to wander in the rose garden. At first Marianne felt self-conscious, as though they would all be watching her, but she seemed to have regained her anonymity.

It took a moment to realise why—they hadn't seen her dance with Prince Sebastian. She walked along the length of the terrace, trying to pinpoint which set of double doors would have been level with where they'd been dancing.

Her concentration was entirely on the ballroom inside when a hand reached out to catch hold of her arm. She looked round. 'Seb.'

'Sssh.' His eyes gleamed in the dusky light and Marianne's stomach somersaulted. He pulled her in close and kissed her. Then, 'Come with me.'

He led her round the side of the terrace and towards a high hedge.

'What's this?'

'A maze.'

The heels on Marianne's shoes sank slightly into the mud. 'I'll ruin my shoes.'

'I'll buy you some more,' he said, refusing to let go of her hand.

Marianne felt an overwhelming need to laugh. 'They're not mine.'

'Then stop worrying,' Seb said as they disappeared inside the privacy of the maze's high yew hedge. He stopped and pulled her towards him. 'I need to kiss you properly.'

She felt his eyes on her lips before his mouth closed the small distance between them. Then his hands moved up to cradle her face.

Marianne's hands pulled him in closer, loving the feel of the full length of his body against her. She know that he *needed* to kiss her, just about as much as she needed to be kissed.

As he pulled away she could feel his smile against her mouth. He was happy.

Seb's hand slid down the length of her bare arm and his fingers locked with hers. 'Come with me.'

'You do know your way through this thing, don't you?' she asked. 'It'll not be good if we have to be rescued.'

Seb laughed.

It was an incredible sound. She hadn't seen him this relaxed since…France.

Hidden at the heart of the maze was a covered seating area. The high hedge walls made it dark and private. Marianne moved a little closer. 'Why are we here?'

Seb pulled her towards the bench. 'So I can kiss you without anyone watching us. Any objections?'

She pretended to consider. 'Not really.'

His teeth gleamed in the darkness and she could see the glimmer of his sexy eyes. 'I love you.'

Marianne briefly shut her eyes against the emotion of that. He'd told her he loved her before. But this time he was doing it as a man, sure of what he wanted.

And he wasn't saying he thought he might be in love with her. Or that he was falling in love with her. He was saying it was a done deal. He loved her. Loved.

Then he moved to kiss her. It seemed as though he was pouring all of himself into it. She could taste champagne and something that was entirely Seb.

She loved him, too.

Seb pulled back and his finger traced her collar-bone and then he picked up the locket. 'I remember this.'

Her eyes shimmered and Seb moved in to kiss her again. He didn't want her to cry. He didn't want her to remember the sad times. The ten years they'd wasted. *He'd* wasted.

If he could kiss her long enough he was sure he could erase all those memories. He was going to spend the rest of his life loving her. Making her happy.

Her hands rested on his chest and he felt her tense and hold him away. 'Seb, what's changed? This wasn't what you said you wanted.'

No, it wasn't. Seb ran a hand through his hair and brought his breathing back under control. His fingers linked with hers and he pulled her towards the seat.

'Is it clean?' she asked, still pulling back. 'I'm wearing cream.'

He gave a crack of laughter.

'What?'

Seb shook his head. He couldn't put into words what he was thinking. But…he loved that strong seam of practicality that ran through her personality. The part of her that had once told him that skinny-dipping was for people who were too disorganised to have remembered their costumes and that bungee jumping was for people without imagination.

'You do know how to ruin a romantic moment.'

'Seb.'

He could feel her frustration and he smiled. No wonder he was confusing her. Seb pulled her onto his knee.

'I'm too heavy,' she protested.

'You're perfect.' Seb let his hand curve round the soft swell of her buttocks and pulled her in closer. 'And I really don't want you to spoil your dress.'

She gave a small gurgle of laughter. 'This is crazy.'

'I know.'

'Gianferro will be angry if I spoil his creation.'

Her neck was so near and Seb couldn't resist pressing a kiss at the base of it and then a second further up.

'Seb.' She said his name on a whisper. 'Please, tell me what's happening.'

'I love you.'

'Seb—'

He raised a hand to place his fingers over her lips. 'And I want you to marry me.' Sure that she wasn't going to speak, he let his hand fall down and he linked his fingers with hers. 'Yesterday I waited with a man while his wife was in surgery...' Seb swallowed down the painful lump in his throat as he remembered how that had felt '...not sure whether she was going to make it through the five-hour operation.'

Marianne sat so still in his arms. He could feel her concentration. 'And he talked about loving her. About knowing that he'd already had more than some people ever get a chance to experience.'

Her hand twitched inside his and he continued, 'And about not having anything to regret because they hadn't wasted a moment.'

'D-did she live?'

'Yes, she lived—and I saw his face.'

Seb turned her chin so he could see deep into her eyes. This was the woman he'd hurt so badly, the woman he'd left pregnant and alone.

The woman he loved.

They had so much to regret. *He* had regrets piled higher than the hedge walls that surrounded them. 'I don't want to waste any more time. Marry me?'

CHAPTER TWELVE

VIKTORIA paced around her mother's private sitting room, before flinging down the newspaper on a low table. 'How completely irresponsible! What were you thinking of?'

Seb glanced down at the front page. He scarcely needed to look to know what would be there.

'How did the cameras get inside the castle?' he asked calmly.

Viktoria almost snorted her rage. 'That is not the point. You assured me there was no relationship between you and Dr Chambers and you're caught on camera kissing.'

'There wasn't.' Seb stood up and walked over to the window, his eyes searching out the guest wing. 'And now there is.'

Isabelle picked up the newspaper. 'She's the woman you danced with last night.'

'Yes.'

'She's very beautiful.'

Seb smiled. 'Yes, she is.'

'Trust you to say something like that,' Viktoria said, turning on her sister. 'The papers have been full of your antics for the last two months and now Sebastian is joining in. No wonder a third of the population think we're an expensive anachronism.'

'Not a third, Viktoria,' their mother interrupted. She reached out her hand for her coffee. 'A small but vocal minority. I do think it's regrettable that this…affair has managed to push all coverage of your good work at the scene of the train crash to the third page, Sebastian, but it's not unsalvageable.'

Seb turned back from the window. 'I'm going to marry Marianne.'

'Have you asked her?' his mother asked in the small hiatus before Viktoria found her voice.

'Yes.'

Viktoria sat down in the nearest chair and covered her eyes with her hand. 'I don't believe this.'

'I fell in love with her ten years ago and I intend to marry her.'

'You're the Sovereign Prince of Andovaria. You don't "fall in love".' Viktoria's voice was laced with contempt. 'You've got a responsibility to your subjects and to your family. You can't marry some money-grabbing English girl who thinks it might be fun to be a princess on some kind of hormonal whim.'

Seb interrupted her. His eyes were fiercely angry, though his voice stayed low and even. '*Dr Chambers* is a serious academic who'll have to make real sacrifices to marry me.'

'And ten years ago she was a slutty English girl who slept with someone she hardly knew.'

'Enough.' Seb ground the single word out.

The Dowager Princess frowned her daughter down. 'It's not impossible, Viktoria. Sebastian has made countless statements over the past four years to the effect that he continues to hope that he will eventually marry for love. Not once have I read anything that suggests his popularity dipped because of it. In fact, the reverse seems to be true. People seem to feel that it puts him in touch with reality.'

Viktoria sat up. 'You're not serious.'

'Perfectly. I think there's a sufficient swell of

public opinion in favour of marrying a commoner to make it possible. Even desirable.'

'Marrying the socially acceptable virgin didn't work,' Isabelle chipped in.

The Dowager Princess shot her younger daughter a look that demanded silence. 'I would very much like to meet your Dr Chambers. But, with a front page like this, you do realise you've made her position here untenable? We will have to make some kind of announcement.' There was a knock at the door. 'Come in.'

'Your Serene Highnesses,' Alois von Dietrich said as he entered. 'Prince Sebastian, if I might speak with you? Privately,' he added as Seb appeared to hesitate.

With a nod at the female members of his family Seb left the sitting room. 'You look like the world has caved in.'

'Yes, sir.' Alois pulled a file from beneath his arm. 'This has appeared in a London paper this morning. I can only assume they started looking into Dr Chambers' background when she first took up residence in the guest wing. I believe they call it investigative journalism,' he added drily.

Seb felt the first tingle of apprehension. Alois

rarely showed emotion, but the other man looked as stressed as he'd ever seen him. 'What is it?'

Alois pulled out the scanned image and handed it across. Seb looked down at what had always been a poor-quality photograph of Marianne. What made it a picture that would be reproduced around the world was that she was pregnant.

'And this has already appeared in the London papers?'

'Just the one paper, sir.'

One paper, but more would follow.

Alois cleared his throat. 'I understand its publication has already prompted a radio phone-in with listeners suggesting what attributes they considered most appropriate for the wife of one of the world's most eligible princes.'

Seb swore softly. He looked back down at the image in his hand. Marianne had told him about their daughter, and he'd thought he'd understood what it must have been like for her, but seeing her pregnant with his child was painful.

Marianne looked so young. Vulnerable. And he'd left her alone. Frightened and alone.

God forgive him.

'The Press office is being besieged by reporters wanting a statement on your relationship with Dr Chambers. And there has been a significant number of comments in our own Press expressing concern that you should have brought your mistress to stay at Poltenbrunn Castle.'

Seb's mouth took on a determined line.

'We need to issue a statement, sir. The Press office have put together some suggestions and they recommend that something is said in time for the six o'clock news.'

Seb gave a brief nod in recognition that he'd heard and then he walked back into his mother's private rooms. 'The London tabloids have been busy,' he said, handing her the envelope.

She looked up questioningly before pulling out the picture of Marianne. She looked up at her son. 'She's had a baby?'

'Mine.' Seb's voice brooked no discussion.

Isabelle sat up in her chair and swore softly.

'Our baby was stillborn on 17th April—'

'Thank God for that!' Viktoria exclaimed and then backtracked when Seb looked at her. 'I don't mean that exactly, but for you to have an illegitimate child would be so difficult.

Particularly if you haven't been supporting it. Very unpopular.' Her voice wavered.

The Dowager Princess stood up and picked up her cigarettes. The ones she kept especially to remind her that she no longer smoked. 'Darling.' She looked at her son. 'There's no way you can marry her now.'

Marianne shut her laptop with a fierce click. She didn't want to see any more. It was exactly what she'd feared, deep down, though where that particular photograph had surfaced from she'd no idea.

But surface it had—and her past had returned to haunt her. They'd been fooling themselves to think that it wouldn't. According to Beth, no one had yet put a date on that photograph, but they would. It was only a matter of time. And what would the headlines be then?

Marianne placed a shaking hand over her mouth. Thank God there'd been no public announcement about any engagement. Nothing done that would compound her humiliation—because she knew Seb couldn't marry her now.

It was impossible. He might love her, but he

loved Andovaria more. It had the prior claim on his heart.

Perhaps she was a coward, but her instinct was to run. She didn't want to have an endless post-mortem. Didn't want to sit with Seb—loving him, aching for him—while he explained why it was no longer possible for her to be his wife.

She understood why.

With immense care Marianne packed her laptop away, twisting the leads into the narrow channel. She needed to go away. Quickly.

But where would she go? Her mind was in complete spasm. She needed to calm down and think. Going home wasn't a possibility. Her house in Cambridge would be completely besieged by reporters.

Her parents' home? Beth's? The Blackwells'? Every place she thought of was discarded for the same reason. And how did she get home anyway? She'd seen the paparazzi gathered outside the castle for Princess Isabelle, who only might be bringing her boyfriend home—what would it be like now?

Was it even going to be possible to walk into an airport and get on a scheduled flight?

Marianne pulled a hand across her face as the panic inside her started to build. She didn't know how to manage this.

She would need to talk to Seb. Perhaps there was some 'safe' house she could stay at until the furor died down? Then she could quietly slip back to England.

And she would need to talk to Peter and Eliana. Perhaps she should do that first? Marianne pulled her case from out of the wardrobe, her fingers hesitating on the zip pull. *She'd let Peter down.* What would he do now? She brushed angrily at the single tear that trickled down her cheek.

She flung open the lid and filled the suitcase with her clothes. Marianne worked quickly. There was probably no need to do so, but she couldn't bear to sit still. She had to be doing something. Anything.

Eventually she squeezed the last shoe down the edge and closed her case. A mixture of shock, panic and anguish rose up inside her like a wave. Marianne placed her hand over her mouth as though that would somehow stop the dam bursting.

What was she going to do?

She went and sat down at her dressing-table stool and put in her simple studs with fingers that didn't want to co-operate. Then she picked up her heart-shaped locket, her fingers closing round it like a talisman.

For ten years she'd clung to it. Taken it with her everywhere she went. Her fingers trembled as she opened the tiny catch and let the door halves fall open to reveal the photograph of Jessica.

Their daughter.

What would have happened now if Jessica had lived? If she were a living, breathing nine-year-old in Cambridge, going to the local school…?

Acting on a sudden impulse, Marianne laid it open on top of her pillow and then pulled her case out into the sitting room. It was time to leave. To draw one clear black line under this part of her life and reinvent herself as someone else.

But first she had to speak to Peter. Tell him that she could no longer be his eyes. Her bottom lip trembled and she caught it between her teeth. Perhaps Princess Viktoria would be so relieved she was leaving quietly that she wouldn't mind so very much?

Marianne banged a fist against her head. *Think.* She had to have options. There were *always* options.

She could dye her hair with one of Eliana's temporary rinses. She could hide in the back of Eliana's car while she drove it through the waiting photographers. Maybe travel back to England on a ticket Eliana bought? Stay with one of their friends…

Options. She just needed to keep calm—and think.

'Would you like a cup of tea?' Muriel Blackwell asked from the opposite side of her large country kitchen. 'You look like you could do with one.'

Marianne shook her head. 'I think I'd like to go for a walk.'

'Some fresh air might do you good,' the other woman said with a smile as she kneaded her bread dough.

Something needed to, Marianne thought as she stepped outside into the country lane that wound its way down to the river. Her escape from Andovaria had been successful, if not very elegant.

No doubt in twenty years she'd find things to laugh about. Being huddled on the floor of the Blackwells' car with a blanket over her, and assorted cardboard boxes on top of that, did have elements of the ridiculous.

But leaving her suitcase behind and arriving at Muriel and John Blackwell's home with not so much as a toothbrush and a clean pair of knickers was more inconvenient than ridiculous.

Marianne climbed over the stile and walked down to the single-plank bench. She liked it here. She liked the peace and the smell of warm grass. She liked to hear the sound of crickets and even the soft hum of traffic far in the distance.

Two days. And she'd deliberately not looked at a single paper since she'd arrived in Norfolk. Refused to turn on the television or listen to the radio. It was like living in a sterile environment. No contact with the outside world at all—excepting Muriel with her warm smile and fairly constant chatter.

'Marianne.'

She spun round. *Seb!*

'They told me I'd find you here.'

He looked gorgeous. Dark jeans and a slim-fitting slate-coloured T-shirt. Seeing him—here—made her want to cry because she'd missed him so much. Wanted him.

'Why are you here?'

His sensual mouth twisted into a half-smile. 'To find you.'

'Why?'

'You forgot this,' he said, holding out her locket by the chain.

She shook her head. 'I left it for you.'

Seb came to sit down beside her. 'Because I didn't have a photograph of Jessica?'

Mutely Marianne nodded. She didn't trust her voice. *Why was he here?*

'I think I'd rather see you wear it.' He placed it round her neck and fastened the clasp.

Marianne could feel his fingers as they brushed against her neck. Her head was full of the day he'd first given her the locket.

'I was thinking we might do something else to remember Jessica.' He stretched out his legs and seemed to contemplate the slow-moving river in front of them. 'I was wondering whether a statue in the formal gardens at Poltenbrunn might be nice?'

She turned to look at him, her eyes welling up.

'You didn't need to run away,' he said gently. And then, 'Don't cry, Marianne. Please don't cry.' His warm hands reached up to brush away the tears that had started to fall.

'D-did you see the photograph? Of m-me?'

Seb leant forward and kissed her trembling mouth. Marianne could taste the salt of her own tears.

'I saw it.' She started to speak, but Seb laid a finger over her mouth. 'It doesn't matter. None of that matters.'

'But you said…'

'I've said a lot of foolish things.' His eyes swept over her tear-stained face. 'What matters is that I love you and I think you love me.'

'Andovaria won't accept a princess like me.'

'Andovaria has no choice. Marianne, I love you and I want to spend the rest of my life with you. If it ever comes to a choice between that and renouncing my throne—I choose you.'

Marianne started to shake her head. 'But—'

'There is no "but". I've made my choice. If you'd stayed you'd have known I'd done it by the evening news on the day the picture of you carrying our baby was first printed in London.'

'D-did what?'

'I issued a statement to say that the baby you

were carrying in that photograph was mine. That I accepted full responsibility for my actions and that I was prepared to step down from the throne if that was what the people wished, but that I loved you and hoped you'd agree to be my wife.'

He pulled a box from the pocket of his jeans and flicked it open. Inside was a platinum band set with five of the biggest diamonds Marianne had ever seen. 'You said you'd marry me.' His eyes searched out hers. 'Will you wear my ring?'

Marianne covered her face with both her hands and tried to bring in enough breath to let her brain function. She wanted to be with Seb so much, but how could she let him give up everything that mattered to him? At what point in the future would he look at her and decide she hadn't been worth the sacrifice?

'I can't let you…'

Seb flicked the ring box shut and pulled her in close. 'And I can't be without you. If you won't marry me I'll have to leave Andovaria anyway, because I'm going to have to live near where you are. I'm going to spend the rest of my life convincing you that you love me too.'

Marianne could feel her resolve weaken as the

warmth of his arms began to seep into the chill of her heart. 'You'll regret it.'

'If you won't marry me, I'll regret it,' he countered. 'We can do it any way you want. I can abdicate in favour of Michael by this evening and we can plan our future in England. You can continue your career and I'll start thinking about what options are open to me. I want you.'

I want you. He sounded so sure. So certain.

'Or we can go back to Andovaria together and announce our engagement. Then we'll spend some time selecting the sculptor we want to create a statue in memory of our daughter.'

'What will people say?'

'They'll say a lot, because that's what people do. But it's not their life. Only you and I can decide what will suit us best. Make us happy. And I know I can't do another ten years without you.'

A soft sob broke from deep within her.

'I love you.'

Her fingers clutched at his T-shirt.

'We're in this together. And, honestly, I don't really mind what does happen as long as I'm with you. Whatever public opinion says or doesn't say, we're going to be happy. As happy as we would have been if I'd stood my ground at nineteen. Marianne, will you marry me? Have children with me? Spend your life with me?'

Marianne thought of all the reasons she should say no—and then she thought of the one reason she should say yes. 'I love you. I do love you. I've always loved you.'

Seb lifted her chin so she had no choice but look into his eyes. 'So which way are we going? Towards Andovaria? Or away?'

Strong, calm, loving eyes. And she'd no doubt that he meant every word. The choice was hers. If she didn't feel strong enough to face the 'slings and arrows' that would no doubt come their way, maybe even rejection by his country, he'd come with her.

'Andovaria,' she said, huskily. 'If they're prepared to give me a chance…'

Seb reached into his jeans pocket for the second time and pulled out the ring box. 'Do you like it?'

Despite everything, or perhaps because of it, Marianne felt a sudden gurgle of laughter. 'I love it.' She took the box from his fingers and opened it. 'It's beautiful.'

Seb pulled it from its slot and reached for her left hand. 'Mine,' he said, sliding it onto her third finger. 'You belong to me now. Whatever happens.'

He reached across and stroked a finger down the side of her cheek, before his hand moved to thread through her hair. Then he pulled her closer, his lips meeting hers in a kiss that seared deep into her soul.

EPILOGUE

DESPITE the snow, the crowds were at least five people deep all along the route to Poltenbrunn Cathedral. Thousands of flower arrangements had been brought in to decorate the streets and there were streamers and banners everywhere she looked.

It was the strangest sensation to know that they were there for her—her and Seb. Wishing them well.

And her tiara felt heavy. She'd spent the last two months practising walking in it and it was harder than one would imagine. As was the royal wave. Seb seemed to manage something with a flick of the wrist, but hers still needed work.

Her father smiled across at her. 'Nervous?'

'Just a little.'

He leant over to grip hold of her hand and Marianne felt a surge of love towards him and her mother. Her parents had made mistakes, but so had she. She was just grateful they were here.

The glass-topped Rolls-Royce Phantom IV stopped in front of the steps leading up to the cathedral and she was aware that millions of eyes would be watching her climb out of the car. Pencils across Europe would be poised to begin the race to see how quickly they could get a copy of her dress in the shops.

She drew a shaky breath. But none of that mattered. What mattered was the man waiting for her inside. The man who'd been prepared to give all of this up for her—because he loved her.

Marianne stood still while the dress designer moved about her, first adjusting her antique silk veil and then the five metres of train that would stretch out behind her down the aisle. The off-white silk had been covered in Andovarian embroidery, all done by hand and exquisitely beautiful.

But none of it mattered—just the man.

She gripped her bouquet of white roses and sweetly smelling lilies of the valley and walked through the doors to Poltenbrunn Cathedral. Lights were flashing everywhere in bright bursts all around her and camera crews were catching every expression she made.

Behind her she was aware of Isabelle and Beth organising the fourteen young bridesmaids chosen from old aristocratic families. Every detail had been thought about, planned with military precision.

But, none of it mattered. As the organist struck the first chord Seb turned. So far away, right down by the altar, waiting for her to walk towards him. He smiled and her nerves vanished.

Dressed in full military regalia he looked every inch the prince he was. *But it didn't matter.* She was marrying the man. For better, for worse. Whatever life threw at them, good or bad.

Seb's eyes never wavered from hers as he watched her make her way towards him. Marianne didn't notice the crowned heads of Europe and beyond, the politicians and diplomats that sat in the pews. She didn't even notice the carefully chosen white flowers and green plants that decorated an already beautiful cathedral.

Just Seb.

And then, as she came level, he reached for her

hand and his smile told him how much he loved her. Would always love her.

Marianne had been nervous about so many elements of the day, but Seb was right. In the event, she forgot the millions of people watching every move she made, all she could see was Seb.

She felt him slide the unbroken platinum band on her third finger. Her German was slightly faltering, but nothing had ever felt more right than sliding her ring on his hand. Heard the moment they were pronounced husband and wife.

Marianne moved dream-like through much of the service, but she would always remember the moment she signed the register. 'My princess now,' Seb whispered quietly.

Princess Marianne of Andovaria. Strange. A new life. New responsibilities and challenges. But whatever they were, Seb would be right alongside her.

He took hold of her hand and tucked it in the crook of his arm and led her out of the cathedral in a peel of bells. Marianne heard the cheer go up like a wall of sound and then a more distinct, 'Kiss her.'

Seb turned towards her and she could read the

intention in his eyes, the deep glimmer of pride and sheer joy. 'Your mother said to wait until the balcony,' she whispered.

His smile broke forth. 'Yes, she did, didn't she?'

Marianne knew he had no intention of waiting when his eyes flicked to her lips.

'I love you.'

To the sound of cheering, Seb bent his head and kissed her.

MILLS & BOON® PUBLISH EIGHT LARGE PRINT TITLES A MONTH. THESE ARE THE EIGHT TITLES FOR JUNE 2007.

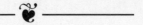

TAKEN BY THE SHEIKH
Penny Jordan

THE GREEK'S VIRGIN
Trish Morey

THE FORCED BRIDE
Sara Craven

BEDDED AND WEDDED FOR REVENGE
Melanie Milburne

RANCHER AND PROTECTOR
Judy Christenberry

THE VALENTINE BRIDE
Liz Fielding

ONE SUMMER IN ITALY...
Lucy Gordon

CROWNED: AN ORDINARY GIRL
Natasha Oakley

MILLS & BOON®

MILLS & BOON PUBLISH EIGHT LARGE PRINT TITLES A MONTH. THESE ARE THE EIGHT TITLES FOR JULY 2007.

— ❦ —

ROYALLY BEDDED, REGALLY WEDDED
Julia James

THE SHEIKH'S ENGLISH BRIDE
Sharon Kendrick

SICILIAN HUSBAND, BLACKMAILED BRIDE
Kate Walker

AT THE GREEK BOSS'S BIDDING
Jane Porter

CATTLE RANCHER, CONVENIENT WIFE
Margaret Way

BAREFOOT BRIDE
Jessica Hart

THEIR VERY SPECIAL GIFT
Jackie Braun

HER PARENTHOOD ASSIGNMENT
Fiona Harper

MILLS & BOON®

0607 Rom LP